# FROM THE HORSE'S MOUTH

## A JAILER'S TALE

By

Bill Bradshaw

A Story of Jesus, Jailers and The Juice

Cover photograph by Phil Seabrook
Photograph taken in Millmount House Dublin.

'All persons in this book are fictitious and any similarity to persons living or dead is purely coincidental.'

© Copyright 2004 Bill Bradshaw. All rights reserved.

No part of this publication may be reproduced, stored in a retrieval system, or transmitted, in any form or by any means, electronic, mechanical, photocopying, recording, or otherwise, without the written prior permission of the author.

Printed in Great Britain, by Cox & Wyman Ltd

Note for Librarians: a cataloguing record for this book that includes Dewey Classification and US Library of Congress numbers is available from the National Library of Canada. The complete cataloguing record can be obtained from the National Library's online database at:
www.nlc-bnc.ca/amicus/index-e.html
ISBN 1-4120-2443-9

## TRAFFORD

This book was published on-demand in cooperation with Trafford Publishing. On-demand publishing is a unique process and service of making a book available for retail sale to the public taking advantage of on-demand manufacturing and Internet marketing. On-demand publishing includes promotions, retail sales, manufacturing, order fulfilment, accounting and collecting royalties on behalf of the author.

Suite 6E, 2333 Government St., Victoria, B.C. V8T 4P4, CANADA
Phone 250-383-6864   Toll-free 1-888-232-4444 (Canada & US)
Fax 250-383-6804   E-mail sales@trafford.com   Web site www.trafford.com
TRAFFORD PUBLISHING IS A DIVISION OF TRAFFORD HOLDINGS LTD.
Trafford Catalogue #04-0271   www.trafford.com/robots/04-0271.html

10   9   8   7   6   5   4   3   2

*In memory of Brian and Edel
Clocked out before the shift was over.*

*Very special thanks to Ter and Doris, Maurice Matthews, Phil and Paul Brennan, Mag and Val, Big Brian McAuley, Martin Beegan, Neville Thompson, Bob and Victor Bradshaw, Ger Bradshaw, the lovely Miss O Connel, Shane Kelly, Ian Guildea, Keith Rogers, Mick O Mahoney, Norman Sharpe, Mick Fitz, Group 18 and to the men and women of the Irish Prison Service who have made my life a better place to be.*

*For Laura and Jack*

## ABOUT THE AUTHOR

Bill Bradshaw was born in the backseat of a Fiat motorcar on the 7th of November 1966. He grew up in the tumbleweed town of Rathkeale in County Limerick, and headed out into the world to find his fame and fortune in 1986. Spectacularly unsuccessful, he returned to Ireland in September 1989, and found a friend in Dublin. In an act of pure charity, Terri married him 1994, and he has two great kids that see past his shortcomings. He has been a Prison Officer in Mountjoy Jail since 1997, and served two years as a union representative on the Prison Officers Association. He is prone to exaggeration and has problems with his weight. **'From The Horses Mouth – A Jailers Tale'** is his first novel.

# CONTENTS

## PROLOGUE : FOLKLORE AND HARD FACTS
(i) SPECIAL BREW — 11
(ii) DEATHS AND NEW CHAPTERS — 17
(iii) TOUGH TIMES — 19
(iv) OF ROGUES AND RASCALS — 22
(v) A LONG, LONG WAY FROM THERE TO HERE — 25

## CHAPTER ONE: THURSDAY
(i) ANOTHER GREAT DAY FOR THE LADS — 29
(ii) THE DANCING HEGARTYS — 34
(iii) THE SHERIFF OF DODGE — 41
(iv) A NEW ARRIVAL — 47
(v) THE CISTERNS OF CHARITY — 49
(vi) ZEDS DEAD — 54
(vii) COMING BACK — 57

## CHAPTER TWO: FRIDAY
(i) THE MORNING AFTER — 69
(ii) OLD FRIENDS — 71
(iii) THE GOVERNOR — 73
(iv) THINGS CAN ONLY GET BETTER — 77
(v) THE TAVERN — 83
(vi) ROOTS AND RAW DEALS — 89
(vii) THE EAGLE HAS LANDED — 95
(viii) THE TURNING OF THE SCREW — 97
(ix) RIGHT ON CUE — 101
(x) FRIENDS AND DEADLY DUOS — 108

| | | |
|---|---|---|
| (xi) | MAN AND BOY | 116 |
| (xii) | A NIGHT TO REMEMBER | 120 |
| (xiii) | TALBOT | 127 |

## CHAPTER THREE : SATURDAY

| | | |
|---|---|---|
| (i) | BREAKING THE WAVES | 131 |
| (ii) | HE AINT HEAVY | 136 |
| (iii) | IF YOU GO INTO THE WOODS TODAY… | 141 |
| (iv) | POWDERKEG | 150 |
| (v) | COMES THE DARK | 162 |

## CHAPTER FOUR: SUNDAY

| | | |
|---|---|---|
| (i) | THE FUTURE | 167 |
| (ii) | THE LONGEST TIME | 171 |
| (iii) | JESUS, IT'S HOT | 195 |
| (iv) | SO LONG FRIEND | 205 |
| (v) | WHAT WILL BE, WILL BE | 212 |
| (vi) | HOLDING BACK THE YEARS | 219 |
| (vii) | TOUCHED BY AN ANGEL | 224 |
| (viii) | THE LAST ALONE | 235 |
| (ix) | TAKE IT BACK | 240 |

## CHAPTER FIVE: THURSDAY

| | | |
|---|---|---|
| (i) | THE LAST WALTZ | 253 |
| (ii) | FULL CIRCLE | 256 |

## EPILOGUE: TIME AFTER TIME

JULY 7th 1813                                             259

# PROLOGUE : FOLKLORE AND HARD FACTS

(i)  SPECIAL BREW

In the summer of 1810, the rural Irish town of Drumasheen lay hidden from the world at the foot of Dinnegans Hump, in the parish of Clohune. She was unremarkable, even by the standards of rural Irish communities of the day and were it not for the occasional presence of occupying British troops on Lord Richards estate, she would not have appeared on maps, charts or graphs. But that was about to change.

Through August of that year, Paudie Mulhare worked feverishly, preparing a batch of his much renowned and highly respected poitin and, with Christmas fast approaching, he was giving his all not to disappoint his eager clientel. Word had filtered back to him that Connie Hennessys goats had taken to frightening locals who had come in contact with them. Not that they had become violent, but that they were prone to fits of dancing, followed by bouts of intense staring, then convulsive laughter and back to dancing again. Seanie Mulhare had confided in Paudie that, following a nights revelry at the Widow McCormacks house, he had found himself in a romantic clinch with "dat big wight wan". At a highly inopportune moment, the animal had jigged and reeled away from Seanie, leaving his genitals unattended and to the elements. Paudie would play detective and locate the source of such gaiety. He had to have it.

He staked out Hennessys field and watched. In the morning the beasts were docile but, as the day passed, the goats spirits greatly improved and, by late afternoon, they were in party mood. Beautiful sounds bleated onto the evening air and were carried afar. Great crowds gathered to sing and dance and drink and make merry with the herd, and the rhythm of bodhrans and fiddles and tin whistles throbbed into the early hours. The following morning Paudie came again. This time Paudie trailed behind the goats as they staggered about, tired from their nights excess. And then... it happened. Paudie noticed that the creatures ate copious amounts of little, pointed mushrooms that grew in clusters. They gobbled them, nobbled them, ravaged them and savaged them. They couldn't get enough of them. Paudie had found his secret ingredient. His still would be legendary. He spent the rest of the day gathering them wherever they grew. Hennessys field, O Shaughnessys, Murphys, Christ they were everywhere and, regardless of where they grew, they ended up bobbing and weaving in the poitin mix.

"Gifts from the little people" thought Paudie, "Gifts from the little people to make the big people more gifted"

In the early days of November, in the year of our lord eighteen hundred and ten, in the town of Drumasheen, in the parish of Clohune, Paudie Mulhare proudly released his finest ever brew of uisce beatha to an unsuspecting public. By the middle of that month, the first visions of Christ had occurred. Bridget Casey announced to the parish congregation, that whilst emptying her chamberpot out of her bedroom window, she had heard a yelp and when she looked outside, there he was, arms outstretched, in a pool of thick sweat, Jesus Christ the saviour. The church emptied and the insanely pious flock scurried to the holy spot. Despite the overwhelming stench of urine, a decade of the rosary was said and freshly picked flowers were laid. Seanie Maguire would later question the virtue of the place, stating that on the very same night and on the very same spot, a bucket of piss had been thrown over him by a hideous banshee, her eyes burning red and her hair alive with demons. But his trauma went unnoticed, for the good lord had come to Drumasheen, and there would be drink and celebration, and things would escalate.

By the end of November, Christ was truly everywhere. He had been seen leaving the local tavern on several occasions, he had purchased tobacco in Quinlans, he had been seen sleeping in Murphys field and he had stopped to empty his bladder against the gable end of the widow McCormacks house but was asked to stay for dinner, and he did. There were reports of a lake monster in lough Oisin, wavering houses would appear and then disappear on shimmering roads, locals would be seen to sprout extra heads that would argue and fight and abuse onlookers, only to vanish again, but Paudie was busier than ever and the fungus laced poitin flowed like a spring. But it was the religious element that alarmed the authorities. Word had spread. News of gods fondness for Drumasheen was carried north and south, east and west, from Galway to Dublin, from Donegal to the other place... and traders had brought it oversees. By January of 1811, throngs of fanatics, foreign and native had descended on the town, eager to pay homage, and this was very bad news for the British, protestant landowners and forces there. They greatly feared that such an influx of papists would undermine their control, perhaps even quash it.

Their concerns were relayed to parliament and responsibility was laid at the feet of the Lord Viceroy of Ireland, Lord Finchley. He was an astute man, and knew that any attempt to forcibly contain the Christ epidemic could lead to an international incident. So he decided to embrace it, or at least be seen to do so. He had a nephew, who was a vicar in the small hampshire community of Fortborough, and he would send this man, this priest, to Drumasheen to co-ordinate the Christian adorations and, perhaps, expose this charade for the hoax that it surely must be.

The reverend vicar Archibald Meadowvale was a puritan. He terrified his flock with hellish tales of fire and damnation and he kept his vices minimal. He had a great liking for his housekeepers knickers, and he insisted that she washed her undergarments at the rectory. There, he could investigate them for the scents of satan and, in doing so, keep Mrs. Crabtree free from the fingers of the devil. She appreciated his commitment to her salvation, but always washed her lingerie again when she got them home.

The good vicar was despatched to Drumasheen in March of 1811, and was welcomed by An Cairde Na Dia, the friends of God, on his arrival. He attended a function in his honour and, though not a drinking man per say, he sampled a glass of Mulhares tipple to be sociable. Six months later, Lord Finchley receieved an almost incoherent report from the vicar, stating that the craic was mighty, that Jesus dropped in occasionally, that leprechauns were tremendous athletes and he finished up with a request that Mrs. Crabtree contact him immediately. When Finchley visited later that year, he found Archibald by the local tavern fireside in frantic conversation with an empty barstool, laughing and indicating that his glass needed refilling. He was dressed in a ballgown and wore spotted bloomers on his head.

On noticing Finchley, he got up, smiled and asked the Lord Viceroy to pull his finger.

Finchley knew that Archibald could not return to English shores, as questions would of asked about the Viceroys choice of ambassador and, likewise, he knew that the vicar, who now wished to be referred to as Madame Crotchley, could not remain as spiritual liason to the ever growing masses. So, he bestowed lands and titles upon Archibald and made him Lord Meadowvale. Once back in England, he heralded the feats of the vicar, saying that he had indeed immersed himself in the mood of the moment and, that in recognition of his great effort, the area once known as Drumasheen would now, officially, be recognised as Meadovale. And so it was, that the town of Meadowvale was born.

(i)    DEATHS AND NEW CHAPTERS

The 7th of July 1813 was a particularly bad day for Paudie Mulhare. He had spent the day sampling his latest brew and, shortly before 9pm, he answered a knock on his door to find his long deceased father, Moses Mulhare, glaring back at him. Moses was unhappy that Paudie had taken to washing himself weekly and trimming his hair accordingly. He felt that Paudie was now very much the businessman, and he carried the filthy trappings of commerce on his person. The Mulhares were dirtfarmers and proud of it, and the sweat of the body and the chaos of the gruige were statements to the world that you were a real man, a Mulhare man. Paudie tried to explain that he was catering to a more cosmopolitan market these days, but a terrible fight ensued and in the scuffle, Paudies heart gave in and he passed away to continue the debate elsewhere. It appeared that the secrets of the still passed with him also.

His funeral was a gala affair. Mourners came from as near as next door and as far away as Madrid. Lord Meadowvale himself attended, dressed in a red laced burlesque number and, afterward, the local people talked about the touch of class that the aristocracy had lent to the occasion.

In 1816 a mill was commissioned for the town, and it's construction provided employment, not only to the townland, but to hamlets and villages for many miles. On it's official opening, a poorly Lord Meadowvale made one of his last public appearances and stated that it marked a great new chapter for the area and, that soon men from other worlds would navigate the vast oceans of space to marvel at this achievement. But the darkest episode of Irish history was just around the corner, and the beautiful, innocent peoples of Meadowvale would be swallowed up by it... as would so many others.

### (iii)   TOUGH TIMES

In the spring of 1847, local farmers began to notice the onset of a potato blight. Black balls of sludge were being pulled from the earth where healthy new pratees should have been, but although it was a matter of some concern to those who were pulling, it was not unusual for a bad month of harvest to occur. Late frost very often affected the quality of potatoes, as had happened in '29, and that had sorted itself out by summer. But this was different. By October it was evident that the years crop had been lost to some unseen evil, and farmers prayed that this was a once off. But, Paudie Mulhare was dead and Jesus didn't live in Meadowvale any longer. 1848 was worse and, just when it seemed that things had descended to their limit, the Great Famine, that bastard plague, that hand of death, stretched it's rawboned fingers over Ireland and squeezed... and the dying started.

*The hedgegrows were garnished with sadness and cloth,*
    *torn from the children that lay on the grass,*
    *their innocent eyes, tears frozen and still,*
    *welcomed the face of death as he passed.*
    *Fathers with corpses laid on their backs,*
    *Carried their heads by their hearts beating low.*
    *Mothers with rosary beads asked of themselves,*

*where did the Jesus of Meadowvale go.*

So wrote the poet Arthur Kane when he passed by the township in the almost arctic winter of 1849, but words could never truly capture the horror, the sadness, the loss that was Ireland in those awful days.

People died and were glad of it. Whole families passed away in stinking, rat infested hovels, each one lamenting the loss of another. And their passing was not silent. The once quiet and peaceful landscape was stained with bile and suffering in the slaughter of a nation. The blight had done what England could not do and, for her part, Britain turned away. She was busy forging links with the new world and fending off the threat of the French. Of course, she did make available the condemned vessels, the coffin ships, of her naval fleet. Ships that were destined to sink miles from the Cornish coast, like empty leviathans, now sank miles from the Irish coast, like nautical tombs interring the thousands of weary buachaills and cailins who had dared to dream their dreams of a new life in the west.

Needless to say, the mill was closed. It stopped production in 1850 and, by order of parliament, it was re-opened in 1851 as a workhouse. This was done to prevent the spread of diesese to bloodstock from the roaming afflicted. Families were admitted and then segregated, male to male, female to female, and most who passed through her gates, captured the last image of their loved ones and their homeland, for the history of such places would suggest that they would not see either again. History did not lie. In a population census taken in 1838, it was shown that Ireland had in the region of nine million inhabitants. By 1855 that figure was three million. Almost 100 years later, a crazed Adolf Hitler would perpetrate a similar crime against humanity, only this time the world would take notice. But for now, at least , the famine was over.

(iv)  OF ROGUES AND RASCALS

In the years that would follow, it was inevitable that crime would become rampant. No gentleman or lady was safe in the countryside, and pocket-watches and brooches became currency. Roving gangs descended on factory wagons and an era of legend was born. Stories of highwaymen and thieves, of rogues and rascals, abounded in the circles of Londons elite and, the fleet street hacks, quick to spot a market, got themselves to places like Meadowvale in search of the 'truth' behind the Dick Turpins of Irelands highways and byways.

For the price of a fine whiskey, tavern locals recounted the exploits of such colourful characters as Wild Willie B, who would jump, naked, in front of coaches and dazzle the horses with the size of his sexual organ. After that, the occupants would hand over their valuables for fear of a rodgering, and Wild Willie B was away. Then there was Mad Mo Of The Mountains who, legend had it, had been presented with a magic stick by the little people that afforded Mo the ability to shapeshift. Regularly, so the story goes, he would be seen as a bat stealing necklaces, or as a squirrel sweeping from the trees to remove the hats of the gentry, but mostly, he appeared as a battered old whore who would spread venereal diesese to British soldiers in punishment for the occupation. Most notorious of all though, was Remorseful Phil, who would mask his face with ladies hosiery and relieve the aristocracy at gunpoint. Throughout the ordeal, Phil would fondle himself beneath his tunic, and hisstocking stretched features would twitch and grimace, as his breath crackled and strained to the disgust of his terrified victims. Generally, his hat would fall off at some stage and, following his trademark shudder, Phil would apologise, return the booty and burst uncontrollably into tears, blubbering the words "daddy, daddy" as he rode off into the night.

Sometimes these men of myth would team up. In 1861, Lady Farnsworth reported being robbed by a man who had a hamster sitting on his nine inch penis. Later that same year, a troupe of Italian diplomats had items returned to them by a bawling highwayman, who was seen to be consoled by an old hag sporting whiskers.

In an effort to deal with such scoundrels, local authorities convened in the autumn of 1864, and agreed to convert the disused mill into a jail. After two years of rigorous refurbishment, Meadowvale Place Of Detention was opened to the public and closed to it's residents. With a holding capacity of 460, it promised to be a state of the art facility, that afforded each prisoner the time and space to reflect on their wrongdoings and spiritual guidance would be made available. By 1868, however, it housed 823 inmates and the sewage system was not yet complete. As one scholar of the day wrote in his journal:

"Because of that horrendous place, the whole area smells like an unwashed arse".

(v)     A LONG, LONG WAY FROM THERE TO HERE

Like all long standing monuments and institutions, Meadowvale Jail had it's own history. It had five wings , listed as red, yellow, blue, green and black, and it operated off the hub system, as many British built prisons did. Basically, this meant that the wings extended from a central circle like fingers stretched from an open palm. The titles of the divisions had nothing to do with their décor, but were merely in reference to the hue of a convicts complexion after spending a night on the bunks.

In the latter part of the eighteen hundreds, the prison housed mostly drunks and rebels. The Republican Brotherhood, a group of Irish freedom fighters, made home of the red blue and yellow areas, and the drunks slept wherever they passed out. The green and black divisions housed a variety of felons, from sexual deviants like The Farmers Alliance, to the bullies and so-called hardmen of the local gaelic athletic clubs, who would clobber and strongarm those who derived no pleasure from kicking a pigs bladder round a soggy field.

In the early nineteen hundreds, the jail was home to more rebels, who had dropped the Brotherhood in exchange for Army and who, following 1916, would constantly complain about the state of the countrys postal system, as letters would spend eons in transit to and from the outside world.

The drunks still littered the hallways, and members of The Homosexuals Against Repressive Regimes Youth Society, or H.A.R.R.Y.S for short, were busy cleaning, dusting and decorating right up until the fifties, when the authorities decided to leave the problem with the church. Subsequently, paedophile priests all over Ireland damned their queer souls to hell.

The sixties and seventies saw the incarceration of the hippy movement and the governors of the day were plagued with letters objecting to the kharma of the institution and a series of well publicised sit-ins took place to demand that the officers remove their communist styled moustaches. And of course there were rebels. During a daring escape attempt in '74, provos told officers to take cover, and the infamous Seamus McHillen proceeded to blow one of the security high gates into the air. Armed soldiers were on hand though, and none of the prisoners actually managed to exit the building.

Later, the organisation would begin to splinter, and along with The Irish Republican Army, there was The Real Irish Republican Army, The I Can't Believe We're Not The Real Irish Republican Army, The Fuck Me, Who Are You Irish Republican Army and The Knit Yourself To Freedom Irish Republican Army, who crafted lovely sweaters with Christmas trees and Tiocaidh Ar La weaved into them.

But a more sinister element surfaced in the late eighties and nineties with the onslaught of the drugs epidemic. Filthy, wretched creatures gimped about the prison, and there were whispers and shady deals and cuttings and vendettas. The illness was infectious. Men previously of sound health and nought but misguided temper, descended to the levels of beasts. The good work of the H.A.R.R.Y.S quickly faded, and the walls and floors became vomit and spit stained, and a ferocious battle for dominance loomed. The provos were structured and regimental, and they would not share quarters with dirt like this.In 1992, a decision was taken to transfer republican elements to the midlands and, when this was done, all that remained in Meadowvale was the hardline scum that no other institution would have. By 1993 tensions were high, as the prison authorities attempted to curtail the flow of weapons and contraband in circulation. Nets were erected above the prisoners exercise yards to trap items thrown over the walls, and all visits were conducted either side of perspex screens. But in August of that year the place erupted. Led by Sean 'The Beast' Talbot, prisoners rioted and smashed their way onto the rooftops. Prison Officers, ill-equipped and unprepared were sent up after them to fight hand to hand. But the enemy was armed and, following encounter after bloody encounter, the nets were removed, the screens were dismantled and the rabble came down.

Later, prisoners right groups would allege that brutality forced them up there, their families would claim that the state had failed them, the public expected that it was the drugs and the papers printed them all, but the inmates of Meadowvale left in their wake carnage and devastation... and three prison officers were killed in the execution of their duties.

The force would recover but never forget. These raw, battle hardened men and women were resilient, expected nothing for nothing, cared little for the opinion of outsiders, sought solace with their own and, it is here, in the chaotic world of the jail warden, against the backdrop of Meadowvale, at the foot of Dinnegans Hump, that our story is set.

# CHAPTER ONE: THURSDAY

(i)   ANOTHER GREAT DAY FOR THE LADS

Andrew Purcell sat to one side of his bed, in the J.F.K memorial suite of Mrs. Hegartys guesthouse, and fidgeted nervously with his files. He'd been edgy for days in anticipation of today, and he'd woken at 4.30 am in the throes of an anxiety attack that made his heart palpitate, and his bowels surprise him for the first time in over forty years. He had loved his job, and the friends and acquaintances he'd made during the 28 years of 'Purcells Guide To Irish Pubs' had been good ones. But for every high there is a low, and this was the lowest point in the research year.

Today, he would review 'The Percival Richards Bar And Tavern' in the town of Meadowvale. Percival, himself, had requested the inspection, and had offered Purcell expenses and payment for his time. But, it was professionalism and not cash that had brought him to this place, for no amount of money would have sufficed. It really shouldn't have been that difficult. After all, the area was incredibly beautiful and the whole place was steeped in history. The townsfolk were, by and large, good people and hospitality abounded just about everywhere. A small stretch of pavement , where Christ had, apparently, been seen in the eighteen hundreds, had been lifted and placed outside of the town to prevent pilgrims from blocking up the town on creamery days, and there was a mystic flavour to the place that was plucked from an age long since faded with time. But it was also a jail town

and, 'The Percival Richards Bar And Tavern', much to the despair of it's proprietor, was a jailers haunt.

Four years earlier, Andrew Purcell had unwittingly wandered into the bar in pursuit of his trade. It was an experience that he deeply, deeply regretted. Great hulks of men emptied pint glasses in a single swallow, and there was shouting and roaring and profanity so explicit in it's content, that the very echo of it made Purcell blush. And they had hurt him. He had found himself tied to a chair, naked from the waist down, with a tumbler cupping his scrotum, and he was carried, chair and all, shoulder high out onto the street, where he was left at the bus stop with a sign that read 'ANYWHERE BUT HERE' placed around his neck. Later, he would report his ordeal to Sergeant O' Driscoll at the local station. O' Driscoll, a former prison officer, who ate pork pies and scotch eggs throughout the statement, had called Purcell " a sad bastard with no sense of humour", and told him to go back to Dublin and get a life. He lived in Carlow.

Purcells hands began to shake and his files slipped from them and scattered about the floor. He had not believed that he would ever find himself here again. For four full years, he had managed to avoid Mr. Richards calls but, when Percival caught up with him in June, he was assured that a tough new Chief Officer, one Augustine Mulcahy, had been posted to Meadowvale, and that a clean up operation was very much underway. With guarantees of a safe passage from Percy, and his own commitment to his publication, Purcell had agreed to review the pub. He tidied up his things and headed for the tavern.

The main street of the town was busy. Thursday was mart day, and red faced farmers with ugly lumps of stick, tapped cattle on their backs, directing them in and out of traffic. Calves and sheep drifted into shops where they were greeted by locals, who fed them chocolate. Purcell greatly enjoyed this, as it was the kind of scene exclusive to the backwaters of a country now fuelled by the tiger, and he took the time to soak up the atmosphere. After a short recess, he was on his way, and up ahead he saw the grand exterior of his destination. Age dripped from the stonework of the inn, and Purcell thought to himself that it would not look out of place on a postcard to America.

Feeling more confident, he picked up his pace and was admiring the wonderful craftsmanship of the fine oak doors that he passed through when,

" FUCK YOU HORSE !".

Doc Grady was in heated discussion with a horrified looking Percival Richards over beverage measurements. A concert of chaos resonated in Purcells ears, and in a corner of the bar, Paul 'Pablo' Rogers was mounted on a table with his uniform trousers round his ankles, blasting out the chorus of 'Let Me Entertain You', as a banjo and fiddle accompaniment struggled to keep time. Phidelma Gorry and Bridget Darcy clapped and bopped to the rhythm, and all around, blue uniforms in various states of presentation, swayed and rocked. Pints and shorts passed in all directions, and a fog like smoke engulfed the crowd. Doc Grady rose up and once again addressed the owner.

" I said FUCK YOU, now fill the glass up to the fucking line, or I'll come in behind the counter and I swear to god Percy, I'LL BUST YOUR FUCKING HEAD"

and he waved an angry fist in the air to hammer home the point. A large crowd offered encouragement, and with a chant of " Yup, Yup, Yup" Percy conceded and filled the half an inch of ale to Docs satisfaction.

Andrew Purcell skirted through the crowd to the gents in search of sanctuary. When he got there, he found Officer Matty Morris and Assistant Chief Officer Paddy Devoy, standing in an inch of urine, facing a full length mirror. Both men had their genitals exposed and, upon noticing the obviously shocked Mr. Purcell, Officer Morris said

"Excuse me sir, but from where you're standing, which one of us has the biggest mickey?".

Purcell ran through the crowd and out the door, never to return. It was an exit that would later be described as reminiscent of Jodie Foster running from the crime scene in 'The Accused'.

Outside in the bar, Doc Grady was being calmed down by Tony Ennis, who indicated to Percy that everything would be okay. Richards thanked him for his intervention but, when he'd gone outside to compose himself, Ennis leaned across to Doc and said

"Calm down horse, we'll get that son of a bitch later"

It was 1.55pm and, with a jail to run, Paddy Devoy lifted his glass and raised the call

"once more dear friends... into the breach"

and the pub emptied. 'The Percival Richards Bar And Tavern' did not appear in 'Purcells Guide To Irish Pubs' that year.

(ii)    THE DANCING HEGARTYS

The guesthouse was a good shop. It was well fitted out, and customers had little to complain about when they paid their bills and headed back into the world. It was comfortable, and Nora Hegarty had a way of making you feel belonged, even though it was unlikely that you had been there before and highly probable that you would not be again. Meadowvale had little to offer in the way of entertainment and The Stones hadn't played there in years, but the town saw it's fair share of trade from the Jesus chasers, and the shops were kept busy with visitors for the prison. Nora was proud of what she'd achieved, and considering what she had to contend with in her private life, her public face was warm and happy, and she hid her heartbreak well.

Her guesthouse was one of only three in the town. Mick Roches place provided wheelchair access, something she could not afford, and that meant that he benefited most from the disabled tours, and Sheila Hennegans 'Seaview' stood on the outskirts, nearest to the holy road. No one ever understood why Sheila called her home 'Seaview', as Meadowvale was sixty miles from the nearest coastline, she just thought the name was lovely, she said, really, really lovely.

Things had become a little slow on the holy road, of late. The shrine had not attracted huge numbers in some time, and the last confirmed miracle had taken place in 1987, when Boss Keane had gotten the power of his drinking arm back. Claiming that it would be a shame to waste Gods work, he drank religiously until his liver failed in '91 and he got the chance to thank the big fella in person.

Nora was running a dust cloth over the furnishings in the J.F.K suite, when she caught her reflection, and she took time out to admire Andrew Purcells trousers. He had fine taste, and the cut and double stitch told her that they were tailor made. But they did not fit her as well as they might and, alas, the image was a sad reminder that age had found it's way about her. Even with the top button open, the waistband garrotted her midrift and her thighs were smothered in stretched cotton. Still, she thought, they're not bad... not bad at all.

As for his shirts, she could take them or leave them really. Mr. Purcell did not have her stature and she found that some of his garments tugged uncomfortably at her bosom, so she folded them neatly by his bedside and let the summer breeze cascade gently over the great expanse of her semi naked form. She was fingering through Andrews personals, when she heard the jailers passing. They were always up to high jinx, singing songs and pretending to be drunk, and the sound of their banter meant that lunch was over. It was showtime.

Victor Roberts had been Meadowvales undertaker for most of his seventy years. A huge ill-shaped man, the crack of his arse would regularly peer out over his slacks, and the faded rose tattoo that adorned the summit of his left buttock would terrify all those in his wake, a fiercesome sight to be sure. He stood by his oratory window and pressed the binoculars tight to his sockets. She was late. Her bedroom curtains were draped across and, as he inspected his wristwatch under the lens, he thought that he might be caught for time. Francy Magee was stretched behind him, at peace with his maker, and the grieving family would arrive shortly to wish him bon voyage. Victors company slogan of 'We Send Them Off, Heaven Takes Them On' was his guarantee to the mourning that their loved ones were in safe hands, and he told them not to consider it as an undertakers but as a despatch service.

She'd have to get a move on. But he had worried in haste. Nora Hegarty was reliable, if nothing else, and as the paisley curtains rolled back, Victors mind went numb and he was mesmerised.

She ran her fingers through her love trussed mane, holding it high on her crown, and her breasts demanded respect as they struggled valiantly to escape their harness. Her fulsome figure seemed cruelly captive to her garments and, as he zoomed in for a closer inspection, swirls of smoke waltzed from her cigar and played tricks with her features.

"My, my" he whispered "what a gal"

The kind of gal it takes almost sixty five years to perfect. He leaned back to the solemn faced Magee.

"I hate to say it to ya Francy, but you have no idea what you're missin my friend"

Nora Hegarty was swaying to her own rhythm, when Andrew Purcell ran past her door… distressed. At least, he thought himself distressed, until he ran past her door. He stood on the upper hallway of the guesthouse and believed that he could not have seen what he imagined he had seen. But he had. Earlier that morning he had left Nora Hegarty in an apron and a blue rinse. Now, she stood like some Gestapo seductress, some fraulein of the Reich, by her window, dressed only in a bra and trousers… his fucking trousers.

"Sweet Jesus" he gasped, and he backed away.

Upon noticing him, she pulled the curtains closed.

"Ah, Mr. Purcell" she said in her soft country tone "You'll be wanting some tea and sangwidges"

Andrew Purcell wanted nothing more than to be as far away from Meadowvale as modern mechanics could take him, and soon enough he was.

Shortly after he left, Nora was enjoying a siesta on the sofa, when the doorbell rang. She felt it was unlikely to be Purcell, considering the manner in which he left, and she had not expected guests till sometime after five, so she donned her house coat and went to see who it might be. The young man on her doorstep was finely groomed and well dressed. He wore a navy striped business suit and his shoes were polished to an army standard. He carried a briefcase and an air that suggested confidence and authority.

"Mrs. Hegarty" he said "I'm from the health board"

and he introduced himself as David Orr. Nora had made it her policy to always ask the occupation of any potential guest, and she certainly hadn't expected anyone from the health board, but she was not in a position to turn business away, and the J.F.K Memorial Suite had suddenly become available.

"Of course" she said "Follow me"

and she left the door open for him to do so.

"Now, I'm afraid that I'm not quite ready for you, Mr. Orr," she said " but I could prepare some lunch for you, a salad perhaps. If you'd phoned ahead, I could have had a hot meal... I hope you'll understand".

Orr put down his briefcase and sat at the kitchen table before being invited to do so.

"I'm sorry Mrs. Hegarty" he said "but I think it's *you* who dosen't seem to understand. I'm not here about a room, I'm here about your son" A wave of panic came over her.

"Sean" she cried " O Jesus Christ, is okay ?"

Sensing her anxiety, he was quick to reassure her. Sean was okay. He explained that he needed to clarify some issues in relation to Seans wellbeing.

"If I can just establish some facts. Sean was involved in an accident some years ago, I believe, sustained a serious blow to his skull"

"That's right" she said "He was working at O Connors Transport at the time, yard manager you know, doing very well for himself. He was seeing a lovely girl too and they had discussed getting mar… "

But he cut her short.

" Just the details of the accident Mrs. Hegarty, not his life story if you don't mind. Now, he was working in this transport yard and the tailboard of a lorry came loose and hit him on the head, correct?"

She didn't like Mr. Orr at all. He was a nasty man.

"Why are you here sir?" she asked

" Well, not to be insensitive Mrs. Hegarty" he said "but I believe that the accident left him… a little strange. Could have taken gold and silver in the same event at the special Olympics, that sort of thing".

Nora had had enough. No two bit cocksucker in a fancy suit was going to come into *her home* and disrespect her family like that.

"Right" she said "That's it. Sling your hook mister"and she handed him his briefcase before leading him to the door by the collar.

"Your son dances in the street Mrs. Hegarty." Shouted Orr "He's become a public nuisance and who will take care of him when you're gone. I have a health board writ to have your son taken into care, for his own good Mrs. Hegarty."

Into care. She released her grip. INTO CARE.

"What the fuck do you mean... into care?"

He handed her the order.

"We'll be back in a week. Look, this isn't pleasant for me either, but he comes into our custody in seven days, and that time has been given to see if you can make alternative arrangements for him, but, we've done our homework, Mrs. Hegarty, and your on your own.

"We offer the only viable long term option for Sean. It's for the best. Now, I bid you good day."

and he drove off in his car in the direction of Galway. En route, he passed Sean in the middle of the road, with his back to a stretch of angry traffic. He was dancing his way into the town square. Ever since the accident, Sean Hegarty sure did love to polka.

(iii)   **THE SHERIFF OF DODGE**

It was shortly after 3pm, and Chief Officer Augustine Mulcahy was standing in the main circle of Meadowvale jail, hateing the men. They'd been to the pub as usual, the filthy swines, and now they scurried in and out of the wings, escorting prisoners to and from their designated areas. He'd come to the prison three months earlier to fill the vacancy left by Milo White, who had demanded that female officers push him, naked, around the jail in a wheelbarrow during his inspections. He had transferred to Mountjoy on the commitment from the department that wheelchair accessibility would be provided there, and Mulcahy got the call up. They had sent him in because he had promised to sort out the staff, and he intended to be as good as his word. There was a new sheriff in Dodge.

He did not underestimate the task at hand though. Only last month, his authority had come into question, when the junior minister for depression, Avril Heffernan, had paid a visit and had gone on a jail walkabout. Jeers and catwhistles were showered upon her by both male and female officers, and when she approached Tony Ennis and politely said

"And you are?"

he stood to attention and roared

"I am indeed ma'am, thanks for noticing."

It was extremely embarrassing for the ambitious new chief, and he had vowed to take the wind out of their sails as a matter of urgency.

Assistant Chief Officer Leonard Fennell tentatively approached Mulcahy in the circle. Leonard was a quiet, timid man, some would say weak, and he was sadly intimidated by the fiercesome presence of Augustine, but, the call seemed important, so he tugged at the chiefs tunic.

"Phone call chief" he blurted, and he moved away nervously.

Mulcahy deliberately towered over him.

"From who, Fennell?"

"I think" said Leonard, staring into Mulcahys flared nostrils "That it might be from the Taoiseach".

Mulcahy took the call in his office. He wiped away the light layer of dust from his fathers photograph, and thought it a shame that The Cane Mulcahy had not lived long enough to witness this moment.

"Fat little Augustine, da, and the Taoiseach wants to talk to me".

He fixed his tie, cleared his throat and addressed the countrys finest in his most authoritative tone.

"Chief Officer Augustine Mulcahy speaking, and how may I be of service."

Percival Richards was downright angry and he wasted no time.

"Ah, the good Chief Officer, I had a delegation of drunks from your jail today, and one of them, that horrible shit Doc Grady, threatened me. Now, you want to know how you can be of service... BY CONTROLLING YOUR FUCKING PIGS, THAT'S HOW".

Augustine pulled the phone from his ear. "Fennell" he thought "I'm going to kick your arse"

He listened to Percys version of events, and assured him that the appropriate steps would be taken to discipline Officer Grady.

"Of course, I can't bar them" said Percy,

whose bar had the biggest takings in the county.

"After all, if they treat me like this when I serve them, can you imagine what the bastards would do if I stopped?"

Mulcahy agreed to take care of things. He liked Percival Richards. He was a man of culture, an educated man, and educated men deserved respect. Educated... men... deserved... respect.

He closed his eyes and he travelled.

He was nine years old,... a Billy Bunter. His face was pressed against the cold wood of a classroom table, and he stared up at the other boys, sideways. Their fear for him was of no consolation, but, in the years that followed, it did sit well with him to know that, at least, there was sympathy for him in some quarter back then. The cane swished through the air and cut savagely into the soft flesh of his bare buttocks, and, unable to move because of his fathers powerful hand pushing down on him, he cried for pity into the shirtsleeves of his abuser, but none was shown... ever. He could hear the screeching as the cane cut and cut and cut again.

"FAT LITTLE AUGUSTINE... ... FAT LITTLE CALF"

and he opened his eyes with a start to found that he was safe again amongst the killers and the dealers and the shite. He contacted Leonard Fennell by radio.

"Get Doc Grady and bring him to my office" he barked "and when I'm finished with him, Fennell, I'll be dealing with you"

Dinny O Brien was the elder statesman of the prison, having served the great bulk of his thirty years working in Meadowvale. He was the father of a jailer generation, and he was a friend and tutor to men and women in every corner of the force when, as fresh faced young rookies, they had passed through his hands for guidance. He judged them now, not by what they'd achieved but by what they'd endured, and he would be a sad loss to the job when the carriage clock adorned his mantelpiece in a weeks time. Today, he worked in reception, processing prisoners in and out of the jail. After a hectic morning, things had fallen quiet, and he took the opportunity to open the cover of Thomas Healys 'A Hurting Business', and read again the incredible story of that mans life.

Doc Grady, Tony Ennis and Phelim O Toole returned to the workstation from chores elsewhere.

"Are you reading that *again*" said Phelim.

"It demands to be read" said Dinny "I may get used to it, I'll be doing a lot of it from next week on".

And the conversation went on to the great mans retirement.

Phelim reckoned that Dinny would buy a fur coat and a purple felt hat, and open a brothel somewhere, while Tony saw Dinnys future as a hobo, riding the carriages of freight trains the length and breadth of the country. The possibilities were endless. He could polish himself up and be Madonnas Latino dancer, he could set himself up as the sex God of the next great suicide cult, just without the suicide, he could wrestle bears for shots of cheap whiskey in Canadian mountain bars or, indeed, he could take up a career in the movies."It's true" said Doc "You're the fucking head off James Coburn"

and it was true. He was a tall, world weary man whose smile and gentle manner would be remembered long after he donned the uniform for the last time.

The kettle was just about boiled, when Leonard Fennell interrupted them.

He had run about the jail in search of Doc, and there was an urgency in his voice that was not familiar to him.

"Sorry to bother you men, but Mulcahy wants you in his office, Doc, and he's in terrible form."

Derek Grady left for the chiefs station. On the way, he met Matty Morris.

"Fuckwits on the warpath" he said "I'll need a good union man"

"No better buachaill" said Matty
and they headed down the hall.

(iv)   A NEW ARRIVAL

Victor Roberts was putting the final touches to his comb over, when Nora Hegarty rushed into the parlour, sobbing. He had a hell of a time getting her to calm down, but eventually she imparted the story of the fucker Orr, and his intention to remove Sean from her care. Victor embraced her and held her tight, but the news did not come as such a shock to him. He had wondered for some time when this day would come. Sean Hegarty would have been a handful for any able bodied person and Nora was growing weak with age. The strain of her burden was carried badly at times, and it was well discussed in her absence that looking after Sean would kill her sooner or later. Not that he did not feel huge sympathy for the lad. He remembered Sean when he was a fine, strong chap, with everything to play for. A handsome, popular bloke who could mix it with the best of them, but that was a long time ago, and all that remained now was the memory, for the Sean Hegarty that he had known was gone far, far away.

For now, the Sean Hegarty that remained was just up the road. He threw his legs high into the air, while a group of Spanish catholics took snapshots of 'a genuine mad mick'. They laughed at the sight of him, and he laughed back for reasons he didn't quite understand. In the excitement, no one noticed 'The Wheelchair Bus', as it delivered another troupe of hopefuls to the town, and there was no mind paid to retired U.S Army General Bradford Shaw, as he was rolled down the ramp, and was taken to Roches Guesthouse.

(v)     THE CISTERNS OF CHARITY

The chiefs office was dimly lit, but for a table lamp that shone intensely near where Mulcahy was seated. Matty Morris thought that the Augustine looked like a seer of palms and crystal balls, Madam Mulcahy, bearer of bad news only. There was a silence that was supposed to make the men uncomfortable, but they were too busy making shadow puppets and trying to frighten each other in the dark.

"Take a seat Grady" said the chief.

"I'll stand" said Doc "You wanted to see me"

"Well now... would you like me to stand?"

"What you do is your business. You wanted to see me"

"Yes, yes indeed I did", and he glared at Doc "You've been bold"

Mulcahy expected a reaction, but got none.

"Apparently, you threatened to kill a man"

The chief emphasised the shock in his voice for effect.

"Threatened to do away with him, no less"

"And who was my intended victim, chief?" asked Doc.

"Percival Richards" said Mulcahy,

and he relayed the details of his disturbing phonecall from An Taoiseach.

"I'm taking this extremely seriously, and I..."Matty cut him off.

"So what you're saying is... no Garda report was filed, no witness other than Percy has come forward, *you* didn't actually witness the alleged incident yourself, it supposedly occurred
at a time when I, personally, saw Doc involved in a spiritual debate... a great one for the lord is our Derek, and I'm sure all ten contributors would make a statement to that effect. We have a jail full of murders, rapists and junkies and you think that our time is best employed playing word games in the fucking dark... get a grip man for the love a Jaysus."

The conviction of the delivery had numbed Mulcahy, and had left Doc with a wry smile. The chief was blank. Blank and embarrassed. Embarrassed and humiliated. Humiliated, like a fat child whose bare arse bled for a classroom gallery. The stern, pointed features of Principal Mulcahy stared at him from a photograph, faded with years of forget.

"You bastards"

The words gurgled just above a whisper, and for the first time Matty and Doc were aware of the darkness.

"You rotten... fucking... bastards"

Mulcahy rose up from the light, and in the dim, both men saw a vengeance that truly startled them.

His words were slow and deliberate, and directed at Derek.

"I'm going to have you, Grady. You're a disgrace to the service and I'm going to see to it that you and your kind are flushed down the sewer like that shit that you are".

The pause that followed was appropriate. A slow handclap echoed around the bleak, dank walls, as Matty Morris stepped into the light.

"Well, well" he said, full of admiration "Now that's a fucking threat. Bravo chief, you certainly nailed it that time. Menace, intent, witnesses, the whole nine yards. A fine example, I have to say. You have displayed... magnificantly, all the ingredients of a bona fide, soil the fucking cacks threat. You almost had me going... I almost believed you."

And he shook his head in astonishment, and nudged a bewildered looking Doc.

"All the ingredients missing from Percys tale of woe. What a phenomenal way of analyzing the case of the pissed off publican. I tip my hat to you sir"

Mulcahy didn't quite know if Matty was serious or sarcastic, but he had calmed down and he accepted the point.

"Okay then... okay then... Grady... you go. Off with you now, and stay out of trouble".

He slumped into his seat and ran his huge hands across his tortured face.

"Morris... you stay. There's something else we need to discuss".

Assistant Chief Officer Gerard Magner was a jail rat. A wizened little man, who had attained the rank on the back of his colleagues. At one time he had been a union man but, as so many had done, he had traded the confidences of the staff, for the grubby looking stripe on his shoulder. He had property also. Three or four houses that he rented, and a rocky, barren site that he advertised as 'Rio Grande'. Today was Thursday, rent day, and he sat in the officers mess, fingering notes and mumbling to himself. Coins from emptied telephones spilled out everywhere, and three bundles of fifties stood, regimentally, to attention. Business was good. He was just about to bag the change, when Doc Grady walked past, oblivious to him. He watched as Doc stretched out on a row of seats by the toilets, and passed out."Fucking drunk" whispered Magner

and he thought it was no wonder that Gradys wife had left him. Still, he felt decidedly uncomfortable with Docs presence, so he gathered his stash and locked himself in a urinal to finish the count. He was hurried. The beasts would be unleashed at the end of the shift. He'd do what he had to do quickly, so that he could catch Mulcahy and report Grady for being off his post, and, of course, to avoid being there when the others came farting and belching. They'd abuse him no doubt.

He placed the bankrolls on the cistern, and counted and bagged over £300

in loose change. When he was finished, he threw the plastic pouches into a holdall and left. It was a good fifteen minutes before he discovered that he'd forgotten the bank rolls. When he sprinted into the mess, Doc was gone, and when he kicked in the toilet door, all that Armitage Shanks yielded was a dirty bog roll. The cash, over £2000, was also gone, and the graffiti scrawled along the wall read 'THE CISTERNS OF CHARITY' and 'GER MAGNER SUCKS COCK'. The scream that rang out through the officers quarters, frightened grown men to their very souls.

(vi)   ZEDS DEAD

Mick and Ollie Byrne had worked in Meadowvale since the eighties. They had stood together on the rooftops in '93, and they had soldiered together on the wings most everyday since. They were part of the fabric of the place. They had survived farmyard childhoods, and ever since they could remember, they had found an escape in the magic of the movies. They quoted and critiqued through the long hours of a jail shift and, though four years had separated them, they were known to all as 'The Movieland Twins'. To the great annoyance of the less educated, they held whole conversations in moviebabble, and found an appropriate extract for every situation. During the riots, Mick had stood on the slates and shouted to the onlookers below,

"Look at me ma, I'm on top of the world"

On this Thursday evening, they marched up Quinlans Hill to the 'Percival Richards Bar And Tavern'. En route, they spotted Pablo Rogers, standing on the footpath, holding his overcoat out like a matadors cloak. A great stream of urine flowed from underneath. Treading carefully, they approached him. Grunts and groans came from behind the curtain of Pablos crombie.

"How do, partner" said Mick.

Pablo was extremely pleased to see them. He surely did enjoy the banter of 'The Movieland Twins'.

"Ah, gentlemen, gentlemen, so good they named you twice. And would you two fine fellows be off to the tavern for wine and song, pray tell?".

Ollie pointed to the snakelike trail but made no reference to the odour.

"Something wicked this way comes, sir. What lies beneath?"

"I must ask you, good men, to climb now to higher ground, as the unladylike conduct of my friend here, may heighten her blushes and, therein, dampen her zest for sexual pleasure down yonder laneway. Now, I bid you adieu, farewell, goodnight, fuck off and I shall join you nigh on directly, when I shall regale you with tales of my conquest".

As they walked away, Ollie turned to Mick and said in his best John Wayne,

"He truly is the son of God".

Upon looking back, they saw Pablo donning his coat, as Phidelma Gorry crouched over something unspeakable. Outside the tavern, Tony Ennis' Virago 750 was parked by the kerb.

"Whose motorcycle is this?" asked Ollie.

"It's a chopper, baby" said Mick.

"Whose chopper is this?"

"Zeds" said Mick

"Who's Zed?"

"Zed's dead, baby… Zed's dead" said Mick.

**And in they went.**

(vii)    COMING BACK

Martha Fennell stood at the front room window, and watched her husband walk up the drive. She had often wondered how Lenny had made it into the job. One would have to suspend belief to accept that he made the height requirement and, as he fumbled for his house keys in his conservative anorak and sensible slacks, she reminded herself that he was not the burly warder depicted in the news strip cartoons. But she did love him so. A good, decent, caring man who enjoyed the affections of family and friends for his wisdom and consistency, for his honesty and support. Sure, he was a mild mannered trainspotter to the world at large, but she knew the real Lenny, and for that she adored him.

He stepped inside the hallway and removed his raincoat. He greeted his large companion with a cheek to cheek embrace, made awkward by the fact that she was nearly a foot taller than him. He sat at the dinner table and she placed a stew before him. The house was still, but for the sound of Leonards chewing, and the splash of milk as he drank. Now and then, Martha would ask about the events of the day, and Lenny would understate, keeping his commentary brief and droll.

When the eating had stopped, she cleared off the table and they sat in the silence of a twenty year marriage. Eventually, Leonard went to his coat, searched in the pocket and returned. Carefully, he placed an item on the table, and they stared at it without comment. The handcuffs were worn but washed and they offered a demented reflection of Martha, as she leaned in for a closer look. She stared at Lenny and they exchanged an almost sinister grin.

Len growled "Okay big momma, drop yer drawers and on yer pawrs, cause lovin Lennys gonna burn tonight"

The old church of Drumasheen stood tall and stark against the night sky over Meadowvale. It had held the name of the original town in respect of it's memory, and tonight, Dinny O Brien shuffled along it's aisle, past the great oak pews, to the alter. He lit three candles and, as their flames flickered and danced, he made his peace. He came here often, most evenings in fact. It was the least he could do. Those men were his friends, his family, and he owed it to them.

Jim Gilmore was the closest thing to kin that Dinny had had in this life. Of course there were the brothers and sisters that he had shared a house with in the days before the service, but Jim was real family. They had trained together, bunked together, drank together, laughed together and, indeed, cried together when times were tough... together. He had done a lot of that since Jim had gone. It should have been him... that day... on the roof. Should have been his candle not... *his secret*. The words rang out.

"For a friend, Dinny... for a friend".

Francis Hogan had been a trades officer. A good man who had never allowed the degradation of the prison game to dull his nature, and though Dinny had wanted to remember him well, he could only recall his body, all swollen and shattered and dead. And, of course, Brian Furlong, who had only been in the job six months when it happened. He was a boy in a world of men and monsters, and his face haunted Dinny in the moments that were set aside for sleeping. His peach fuzz cheeks stretched in a great countrymans smile, as he climbed the ladder to the roof, waving to Dinny... waving goodbye. Those gallant men, those unsung heroes, those memories now caught him unawares and he shed a tear or two for the days. He blessed himself, ran his fingers through his silver mane, fixed his collar tight to his chin and headed out into the cold night air. Christmas was coming, he thought, as a winters wind tugged at his clothes. Christmas was coming and so were his last days on the force. What would become of him then? A great gust grabbed him from behind and helped him on his way to the tavern. A black storm was brewing.

Doc Grady stumbled in the dark... pissed. He'd been trying to get from the floor to the bed, but always seemed to end up on his back. Now, he was on his feet at least, but as he reached out for a light switch, he lost his balance and crashed through a bedside table, bursting his nose in the process. He felt the warmth of his own blood stream across his face, and he screamed out for help but no one answered. Why the fuck did she have to go. Why couldn't she have stayed. Because you're not worth fighting for, you fucking prick, that's the why. Because you pissed it away on the juice, because you let him fall, you let him die, YOU , FUCKING YOU,YOU. Night after night in that cunt of a place, shift after fucking shift, coming home bollixed or drunk or both, or angry and bitter and twisted. What did you expect, you dumb fuck. He wanted to shout out to the world, but he couldn't. Couldn't get up, couldn't lie down, COULDN'T FUCKING KEEP IT TOGETHER. Lay down and die, shit for brains, lay down and d...

Several thumps rattled the hinges on his bedsit door. He lay silent and still. Several more.

It's her, Jesus holy Christ, It's her. He forgot about the pain and scrambled in the rubble. Somehow, he managed to find his feet. He stumbled headlong into the door and didn't at all mind the collision. He thought only of the chance. The door swung open, and from the musty, tattered hallway, Sergeant O Driscoll stepped into view and said something about going to the station and £2000. The pain rushed through Docs head... and he passed out.

The room was on a slope. Ever so slight, really, and if you were able bodied it might never come to your attention, but when you're wheelchair bound, everything's uphill. Bradford Shaw propelled himself to the window overlooking the street. He manoeuvred his way into place and locked the position. Once the curtains were tied back, he got a clear view of the scene below. A heavy set lady was in the process of defecating on the pavement outside, whilst a heavily moustached, Hispanic type held an overcoat up to shield her from the attentions of two other similarly moustached individuals. Once they had gone, the female and her protector disappeared down a desperately forgotten looking laneway and, from the pitiful sounds that came back, they fornicated. After that, they entered a bar that appeared to be the focal point of the town. A steady flow of large, boisterous men had made it their destination throughout the evening, and Bradford had identified the voices of the fairer sex amongst their numbers. When he queried Mr. Roche as to who they might be, he was surprised to note that the question made Mick so obviously uncomfortable.

"Thems the jailers" he whispered "bastards from hell"

Mick Roche didn't understand the world of the non-civilian... and just how much Shaw had missed it.

On August $2^{nd}$ 1990, Iraqi tanks trundled across the border into Kuwait, in what was later seen as the opening events of The Persian Gulf War. The international community was united in it's condemnation of the move and, following extensive negotiations, a deadline date of January 15th 1991 was issued for the withdrawal of all occupying forces. When the call went unheeded, Operation Desert Storm roared into effect on January 17th. A massive airborne campaign targeted Iraqi bases to pave the way for the ground offensive that was to follow.

On the evening of February 23rd 1991, U.S Army General Bradford Shaw, stood by the banks of the Euphrates river, outside of Basra, and prepared his troops for war. The next morning, they were to march the Highway Of Death that led into the city, and he briefed them on the dangers that lay ahead. Iraq was notorious for snipers during times of combat and the conflict that had raged with neighbouring Iran, had made the Iraqi soldiers battle hardened and savvy. The men and women that stood before the General were well trained, but without the experience of the enemy, they were fresh faced and naïve. Shaw, himself, was an old campaigner and had seen action overseas on more occasions than he cared to recall… literally. He had grown weary of war, and the option of a senior training position at an academy of his choice would be realised as soon as this mission was over.

Although he could identify the moments that led up to it, and had some recollection of the seconds that followed, he never could remember the shot.

There was the intense burning sensation in his lower back, the horrified expressions that returned his gaze, the ground rushing up to meet him, but... no shot. The sniper had been dug in to a small hillside nearby and was, himself, shot and killed attempting an escape.

When he awoke, he was in a hospital bed in Jerusalem. He was told to consider himself extremely lucky that the bullet had only caused minor damage to his spinal chord and, that with time, he should expect a full restoration of his faculties. That he had no sensation in either leg was not an issue for most serious concern. Rest, relax and allow nature and medical treatment to take their course. But nature and medical treatment did not take their course, and when months later, he was still crippled, serious concern kicked in like a mule. X-Rays, scans, surgeons and consultants prodded, pulled and zapped, but still no tap dancing. Eventually, it was established that physically, he was okay. His problems were deemed to be psychosomatic. Basically, the ordeal had made him aware for the first time that he had been only yards from death for so many years and, that for all of the training and battle experience that he had previously believed would protect a General of the U.S Army,

he could be taken out anywhere, anytime, anyhow.

On his retirement in 1995, he was wheeled up to a podium, where he was presented with yet another medal that he would polish again and again in the long days ahead. Time passed. Days merged. The sacrifices he had made for country caught up with him. He was alone. No wife, no family, no hope. So... he decided to backtrack. He spent hours, days, weeks looking up the history of the family he had before the uniform... and it was there that he discovered Meadowvale. His great great great grandfather, one Moses Mulhare, had lived there at a time when the town was called Drumasheen. He had sired two male children, Joseph, who had immigrated to America shortly after independence, and Paudie, whose history was largely unknown. And another thing he discovered, was that Meadowvale had been a home to Christ, and that pilgrims still ventured to a place called 'The Holy Road' that he may wipe away their tears with his love. He sure hoped that the good Lord had an ocean of love, because he had a sea of tears. So here he was now, staring at hope, staring at tomorrow, staring at what had Phidelma Gorry left on the street.

The tavern was packed solid. Jailers of all shapes and sizes bustled about, and Percival Richards darted from one raucous group to another, in fear of his very life.

"Drink horse, fucking wallop and stout" they bellowed, and he obliged. He hated them, but the whores could spend. Mick Byrne had climbed onto the bar counter with his brother. He turned to Ollie and shouted,

"I love you, pumpkin"

"I love you, honeybunny" replied Ollie, and they cocked their fingers, and pointed at the crowd.

"Any of you fucking pricks move, and we'll execute every last motherfucking one of you"

Percy cleared them off with a sweeping brush, and they went, to great cheers and applause from the men. In a corner, someone belted out a version of 'Moody Blue', and it was clear from their appearance that sideburns and ronnies weren't just in fashion, they were *always* in fashion. A cross section of thirty male and female officers from any era of the service would produce a half a mile of moustache, and here they were now, beer drenched and froth stained, as much a requirement of the job as tunics and peaked caps.

Tony Ennis was in company with Dinny O Brien and Pablo Rogers. The twins joined them and the conversation got round to Pablos exploits down yonder laneway.

"She's not much to look at but, like I've said boys, she plays a mean tin whistle" said Pablo.

Paul was a jail hero, a Meadowvale ladies man, and they could sit for hours to discuss his matings.

"Tell me something" said Tony, "Is that thing real, or are you like a Tom Jones with the sock down the trousers?".

"Yes to the first part, no to the second" said Pablo.

"Fuck" said Tony, and he managed to shake his head and down his pint at the same time.

"Has anybody seen Doc?"

"I saw him earlier on" said Mick, "He was out of his head. Christ, that mans gone nuts on the juice. I can't remember the last time I saw him completely sober".

Everyone agreed. Derek Grady had been a great chap at one stage, but the jail had gotten to him, and Jean had gone.

"Still though, that incident with Francie Hogan must have really fucked his head up" said Ollie, "Can you imagine what that must have been like, holding a man over the edge of the jail roof, his life in your fucking hands, you screaming and him screaming back. He watched Francie fall all the way to the ground when he slipped. Jesus H. Christ boys, there but for the grace of God". And there was a solemn quiet. "The place is heating up again, lads. There's a

couple of bad bastards in there that would have us all over the edge. Thanks be to fuck that there isn't a real leader among them".

"Don't talk about that shit anymore" said Pablo, "Jail's jail, leave it in the jail. Now… who's a girl gotta fuck to get a drink around here?" and he waved an empty glass in Ollies face. As the younger Byrne left for the bar, Mick roared after him.

"You were my brother, Fredo... ... but you betrayed me" and he ran up and kissed Ollies cheek.

At that moment, the shouting and singing died down, as Matty Morris, grim faced and pale, called for silence. He stood on a chair and took deep breaths, as he stared into the faces of his colleagues.

"Ladies and gentlemen" he began "I'm sorry to have to tell you this... but... Chief Mulcahy informed me this evening that, despite our best efforts over the last few years, Sean Talbot, that filthy fucking animal, is to be transferred back to Meadowvale".

There was an explosion of sound. Men roared and pointed and banged on tables. Their anger burst out everywhere. Chairs were knocked over and glasses were smashed. Dinny O Brien walked calmly through the melee, to where Matty was trying to control the rage.

"Quiet now" he pleaded "Calm down for Gods sake", but they did not. He climbed up on the chair beside Matty.

"SHUT THE FUCK UP" he screamed, and they did. "Now Matty, when is he to come back?"

Matty took a deep breath and bowed his head.

"Tomorrow" he said, and the place erupted again.

In the murky shadows of a Mountjoy Prison cell, Sean Talbot, jailer killer, instigator of riots, destroyer of lives, sat rocking... ... rocking and planning.

# CHAPTER TWO: FRIDAY

(i)         THE MORNING AFTER

Doc Grady had bad dreams. He was on the wrong side of the bars, looking out. A big boned brute in badly soiled underpants and vest, stared in at him from time to time, before ambling away into the dark from whence he came. Docs eyes opened, left first, and a knife plunged repeatedly into his skull. He was shelled, peeled, rougher than ever. He made it to the bedside and clutched his head as if it might roll away. When he was satisfied that it wouldn't, he chanced lifting it. He was sorry that he did. So much for bad dreams.

    He was in a Garda holding cell. Rock bottom, horse, end of the road. Whatever his crime was, he was only glad he couldn't remember. A key rattled in the cell door, and he would later pinpoint this moment, the moment he faced his own jailer, as the hour that the winds of change blew softly on his troubled soul. Peter O Driscoll stood in the doorway, half dressed. The y-fronts were pure Picasso, stained and pebble dashed, with a pallet of colour. Something indescribable clung to the crotch, and the vest was greased, sweat stained and decorated with the breadcrumbs from a dozen scotch eggs.

They did not meet well. The vest was badly swollen and hung ominously over the poorly filled jocks, as if the exaggerated stomach could drop at any second and drag the scrotum screaming to the floor. From beneath the wildly over brylcreemed crown, O Driscolls eyes travelled blankly over the sorry sight of the good doctor.

"Come with me, son" he mumbled, and he shuffled down the hallway toward the station office. Doc staggered after.

(ii)    **OLD FRIENDS**

Veronica Gilmore walked through the swing doors of the jail mess, and found the place in shit. The floor was littered with the residue of a wild night, and the combined odours of cigarette butts, stale beer, flatulence and fornication assaulted her senses, and sent her reeling backwards. Dotted about the rows of sadly upholstered seating, lay officers in various states of consciousness, some with pornography draped across their faces to dull the attentions of the morning sun. She'd never gotten used to it, probably never would, but that was okay. They were rough, gruff, loud and lewd but they were kind to her. When Jim had died, they grieved with her, and when all of the well wishers had gone, and the silence that remained had threatened to send her with him, they invaded her world, mowing gardens and painting walls and fixing shelves and dragging her laughter from beneath the veil. They gave her a reason to have the kettle on, and, in doing so, they had saved her. So, she took this job, that she may look after them. She cleaned and cooked for the multitude, and through them, she got to live again.

Something unexpected had occurred. Denis O Brien had been part of her life for as long as she had known Jim. She'd married both o them, really, married into them, and in Dinny she'd found a great oak tree to lean against in the dark days of her mourning. But recently, she'd found something else in Denis. A handsome, charming man, a graceful, passionate man, who made her blush and dip her gaze when their eyes met on the lunchtime rush. He made her feel giddy and silly, but she sought him out for just that reason. Without ever having to discuss it, they were courting and tonight, at the Meadowvale Social Club Annual Dance, everybody would know. She was fifty six going on seventeen. She threw open the blinds, to the screams and howls of the living dead, and waltzed a broom into the chaos.

(iii)　　THE GOVERNOR

By 9.30am, business was brisk. Buses and vans carrying that days court list, loaded up with prisoners, and set off, convoy style, to the world beyond the vale. Tradesmen on hoists, yanked the remains of footballs from the jails barbed wire collar, and basic grade officers hurried about their duties with determination. One may not have sensed the apprehension, but it was everywhere. Sean Talbot was coming home, and the dogs on the streets knew the potential. He was an animal, a beast, actually known as 'The Beast'. In 1993, he orchestrated the rooftop riot in Meadowvale, and he was presently doing a life stretch for the murder of Brian Furlong, with concurrent sentences for his involvement in the deaths of Jim Gilmore and Francis Hogan, not to mention, of course, punishments for the crime that had him in custody to begin with. There was already a hardcore element in the jail, and Talbot would be seen as a messiah, a leader, an organiser. This was not good, and demanded the immediate attention of the union.

Matty Morris and Phelim O Toole marched past the jail front, in the direction of the tower. The tower was the highest point in the prison, and it was where the governors offices were housed. Large glass panels housed in the rooms, and allowed senior management a panoramic view of the institution, which was of no concern to the men as they approached. Murtagh Delahunty studied from behind the great eyes of his sanctuary. He had been top dog at Meadowvale for more years than most cared to remember, and it was the general opinion of the uniformed grades that he was one sad bastard. As Officer Jeremiah O Neary had once put it,

"I believe, gentlemen, that the exact psychiatric term for Delahuntys condition is 'Very... Very... Mad".

Morris and O Toole stopped outside the office of governor one. A rhythmic thump broke the silence. Inside, Murtagh, dressed only in a neatly pressed blazer, shirt, tie and black patent shoes, cradled one ankle into his buttock and danced into the air on the other.

"What the fuck is he at?" asked Phelim.

"Exercising" replied Matty, and he knocked on the door. The thumping stopped.

"Yes" came the effeminate voice "Can I help you?"

"Governor, we need to see you. It's the union"

"Just a minute now" and they heard the creak of metal hinges. "Alright, in you come"

The office was a shambles. Files and folders were scattered everywhere. A tall, sad looking plant was decorated with tinsel from some Christmas past, and a giant poster of Joe Dolan grinned at them lovingly, the words ' Knickers to the lot of you' scrawled in marker across the bottom. A pair of navy slacks were crumpled on the desk, beside a series of encrusted coffee rings that were joined together to make a happy face. A large metal locker stood by the window, it's grey door pulled inward to within a few inches of the lock.

"What is it that you people want?" said the locker.

"To see you, governor" said Matty, not even slightly surprised.

The locker got angry.

"State your business, and then fuck off" it demanded, and the door made a valiant attempt to close, but failed.

"We're not dealing with the furniture" said Phelim, and the locker seemed to detect the frustration in his voice.

"Alright then... turn your backs" and both men did.

The metal hinges creaked again, and a belt buckle dragged across the desk top.

"Now, ladies, what can I do for you today?"

Delahunty was sitting behind the table, fixing his tie and the slacks were gone.

They outlined their concerns regarding the return of 'The Beast' Talbot, starting with a brief on the carnage of '93, and emphasising the fears and anxieties of the staff. Throughout the presentation, Delahunty dug wax from his ear, and scrutinised his finger with a scientific curiosity. When they were finished, he jumped to his feet and pointed at Joe Dolan.

"If only you knew the things that man has seen in this office" he said, "and look at him, with his gyrating hips and his lovely hair. There's a lesson in that for all of us, boys. Now... groom yourselves men, and face the world with a smile" and he handed them combs from his blazer pocket. When they had gone, he phoned the Department Of Depression and, after a few minutes arguing the point with a government go-getter, he shouted

"Listen up son, I want this fucking psychopath out of my jail by Monday, or I'll have the shitty boots of the press, dancing on your ambitious little head by noon" and he slammed the phone down. Rockin' Joe approved.

(iv)   THINGS CAN ONLY GET BETTER

Sean Hegarty could sleep for Ireland. At the end of each day, he shuffled to his room and collapsed, exhausted from the polka. He knew little, these days, as to whether he was loved or not loved, he knew only that life was better when he was out there... flying. From time to time, in between the dizzy heights and the drowning depths of his emotions, he had vague recollections of another life, a soft caress, a union bond with... with... someone, but, like déjà vu, it was confusing and often disturbing to him. With limited understanding, he felt lucky that he could just dance away the pain like that, just block it out... a little...sometimes. Sean Hegarty danced a lot. And when he could no longer throw his limbs at the air, he slept, as he did now, this Friday morning, unaware of Nora and Victors presence at his bedside.

She felt uncomfortable with their decision, but she understood that it was for the best. As Victor had said, Sean couldn't fly this week. Who knows what complaint could be made, and they needed every second if they were to resolve this. Christ, a week to keep your child, what a piece of work is man. They'd have to confine him, but to keep him locked up would have been cruel. So, this was it then.

Victor held up the syringe and stared at her, uncertain of her thoughts.

"You're sure about this?" he asked.

"If you are" she replied nervously, and she held his arm for support. "Tell me again what we're doing here. I can't take this in"

He spoke softly, and she was calm.

"This is Bupivicaine" he said "It's a spinal anaesthesia, not unlike an epidural, just a little stronger. It won't hurt him at all, it will merely numb the muscles from the waist down. He spends the rest of this week in a wheelchair, but more importantly, he stays out of harms way. No one will pay attention to another invalid in Meadowvale. I'll administer this each morning. In the meantime I'll make as many phonecalls to my contacts in the health board as I can, and I'll see if I can't find out what's behind all this. You're not to worry, one of us will be with him at all times, and look sweetheart, maybe the rest will do him good"

She agreed. She just needed to be reassured, that's all. When the needle jagged, Sean Heagrty opened his eyes to the first day of the rest of his life.

Garda house coffee is such a poor replacement for painkillers, but Doc Grady took some comfort from it, as he struggled to come to terms with his plight.

"So... I'm not under arrest then" he said to O Driscoll, as the sergeant got dressed.

"Not at all, man. There was no way that I could have left you alone last night, you were outta your head. So I brought you home with me" and he leaned into Doc with a sinister grin "But you're alright, I don't like boys"

Doc wretched at the thought. O Driscoll explained that he had called around to question him on the missing Magner money.

"Would you believe that stupid prick left £2000 on a fucking jail toilet, and then has the balls to make an issue out of it when it goes missing. By the way , he reckons you stole it".

O Driscoll threw a quizzical eye on Derek Grady. "And was it?" he asked.

Doc stared at him from a badly abused head. "Does this look like the face of a wealthy man, 'cause if it does, you can stick the lottery"

"Sure, sure" said O Driscoll, and he tossed a bag of day old scotch eggs on the table. "Dig in boy, they've made a man outta me".

Doc declined the generous offer, but asked O Driscoll why he had been walking around the station house in his underwear.

"Herself don't like me no more, you know" the good sergeant replied "and a gals gotta live".

And Doc remembered why he'd been so drunk in the first place.

It was 1994, and he was on a lads outing to Liverpool. He'd been on the slide for a year, ever since that day on the roof, and the ghost of Francis

Hogan had chaperoned him everywhere. He would see him on the street, or in the markets, or the pub, and the questions would always be the same, "Why d'ya let me drop, Doc, why d'ya let me die?", and he would scream into the distance at a thousand miles an hour, with his bulging eyes locked on Gradys, just like that day in '93. The crowd had gone to Anfield, and he desperately needed to escape from himself, so he asked a cabbie to take him to a house of distraction, and he ended up in 'The Love Nest', where fantasies come real, bollix naked, with a cheap cigar and a bottle of whiskey, just like in the movies. He expected nothing more than a diversion, a detour, but then Jean walked in, and nothing would ever be quite the same again.

She was Maxine, back then, the lovely Maxine, and she had her own story that saw her strip for lager louts and straddle out the last days of her once glorious bloom. The raven hair, that once drew patterns on a summer breeze, now took a colour from time to time, and the pale blue eyes that had enchanted all those *wild young men from the shipyards*, had grown tired and cold and dead. She had barely noticed him, when she walked in, just another bum, but he saw her. Yes sireee, he certainly did. Saw nothing but her. She put a tape in the cassette player, and stripped while it played. As 'The Son Of A Preacherman' reached Dusty Springfield, the lovely Maxine began to sway and, though she did not know it, she reached deep into the remains of Derek Gradys soul.

*'The only one who could ever reach me,
was the son of a preacherman'.*
And Maxine moved,
*'The only one who could ever teach me,
was the son of a preacherman'.*
through the dark.
*'Yes he was, he was, oohh he was'*
Doc faded, allowed himself to drift, as they made eye contact.
*'Being good isn't always easy,
no matter how hard I've tried'*
And he was on his feet, moving with her.
*'When he started sweet talkin' to me,
he'd come and tell me everything is alright'.*
And she was aware of him for the first time. She saw past his swollen, hurted eyes, past his decay. She saw his sadness, felt that he saw hers. They recognised each other, found each other... and they forgot. Together... Naked... Together. And the only boy who could ever reach her, was a sweet talkin' jailerman, stealing kisses from her on the sly, takin' time to make time, sayin' baby you're all mine, learnin' from each others knowin', lookin' to see how much they were growin'. And in the broken arms of a brothel suite, Derek Grady and Jean Cooke, the lovely Maxine, cradled together, while outside in the evening drizzle, he imagined, Francis Hogan would be waiting with questions.

But that was a lifetime ago and, with a promise to return to the station to give his statement, Doc Grady headed out to face the world... alone.

(v)    **THE TAVERN**

The one thing that Percy admired about the men, other than their ability to deplete his stock and replenish his till simultaneously, was their incredible speed of movement. For individuals who could take eons to meander to the mens room, they could be back at the bar, howling abuse, before the toilet had stopped flushing. Or if he had a beer promotion, or maybe the ever popular 'plate of auld sangwidges', the fuckers could appear from the shadows like psychopaths, clawing and ripping for the drips and the crumbs. With that in mind, he avoided happy hours and complimentaries, not because he was too mean, but because he was too afraid.

They had ruined his life, of that there could be no doubt. He had bought the building in the eighties and, with the proceeds from the sale of the great estate, he began his long, lingering love/hate relationship with the tavern. By the time the debts from the manor were cleared, there was enough left, he felt, to forge ahead with his dream of commanding a centre of excellence for cuisine, fine wines and culture. He imagined that gentlemen of breeding and ladies of good standing, might sit by his fire on wintry evenings and, staring at the flames through raised brandy glasses, they may be encouraged to exchange tales from the good old days, when etiquette and social graces were the cornerstone of any such affair. It would salvage a last link with the world he had known when life was gay, when horseshoes tap danced on cobble stone courtyards... when things were better.

No expense was spared. The woods were from Europe, rich and dark, the carpets, Italian, deep and red, and the cut glass and grand oil paintings were carefully commissioned to replicate the atmosphere of an age long since past. When it was finished, he could have been standing in the great halls of Windsor. Before he threw the doors open on that first night, he stood alone, and allowed the tobacco aroma from his meerschaum pipe to drift into the rafters, where the ghosts of his ancestors, watched with pride. It was invitation only, of course, and by 9pm, the bar was busy with the talk of point to points and jodhpurs. There were toasts to the proprietor and well wishes for the future. Commitments were made regarding conferences, and Christmas menus were suggested for the deluge of bookings that would, no doubt, come. And then... then it happened. The sanctuary was breached.

They descended upon them, like the demon mariners from John Carpenters 'The Fog', strange, wraithlike creatures from the dark, mumbling in voodoo tones. The silence that befell the hall was terrifying, and when they erupted with the blood-curdling chants of " DRINK HORSE... FUCKIN' WALLOP", the scene that followed was nothing short of cinematic. Hysteria caught hold of his gathering and, amidst the screams and the gasps, they left by exits, windows, restroom air vents, the lot. The gentry, the breeders, the business men, yes... even the ancestral ghosts escaped where they could, and all that remained for Percival Richards, were the warders, and it was "drink horse and fuckin' wallop' forever after. Now, the only cuisine to pass his counter was dry roasted, and the best response that he could expect to a glass of fine Napoleon brandy was "Jaysus, dats fuckin' crackin'... now, horse, pass on dat bottle".

The phone was on the far side of the bar, just out of reach, and any break for freedom through the front door would involve navigating the clutter of security locks. Death would surely have him first. Percy crouched behind the pool table, a cue shaking in his hands. He had come down stairs to tidy the place before Friday opening, and was horrified to find that he had burglars. Initially, he was aware of only one, rattling about in the gents, probably attempting an exit, but as he made his way to contact the Gardai, there was some movement behind the counter, and he heard the clinking of bottles. One smashed on the floor. He would have to address them, frighten them perhaps. He swallowed hard and mustered up as much courage as his sphincter would allow.

"I've got a gun" he yelled, and he brandished the cue in the air, "and I'm not afraid to use it".

Nothing. He thought that he was best off reasoning with them.

"You chaps might get hurt" he said "Prison officers drink here, and they'll batter you if you go inside"

He heard a loud moan coming from the toilets. "He's hurt" thought Percy. Perhaps there had been an altercation over the spoils, and one of the creatures was injured. He certainly sounded in great distress. If he was to have a fighting chance, Percy would have to even the odds, and that meant dealing with the wounded animal first. He reinforced his grip on the cue and slipped quietly into the bog.

A cubicle door was closed and the enemy lay within. Pitiful wails broke the restroom silence. "Christ" he thought "this one's dying". Twenty four hours earlier, he had been hoping for a thumbs up in the pub guide, now he ran the serious risk of having a corpse on the premises. He would never hear the end of it from those filthy screws. He would have to resolve the issue immediately, so that this man could expire elsewhere. But first, he would have to overcome them. He wasn't taking anything for granted. He raised the pool stick high in the air, and he kicked in the cubicle door.

The figure that slumped on the toilet bowl paid no heed to the interruption. The head rested on the exposed knees, and the trousers and ghastly underpants graced the urine spattered floor. There was an intense stench, that clawed at Percys eyes and nostrils, hampering his breathing and causing him to cough. Still no movement from the intruder.

He lowered the cue, and aimed the tip at the bleached white thighs, which he poked twice. The creature shuddered violently, and the high pitched howl of a bodysnatcher came forth. Percy retreated in horror, but it was too late. The it thing lunged forward, and before Percy could fend him off, it had him.

"FOR FUCK SAKE, PERCY, I'M TAKIN' A SHIT" it roared, and they wrestled. Richards managed to break free, and he burst through the door into the bar, only to run straight into the animals accomplice. It was all too much for Percy, and he fainted.

Mick Byrne shuffled from the gents, failing miserably to get his drawers past his knees. Outside, Ollie stood with a freshly opened bottle and a half empty glass. Percival Richards lay at his feet.

"That fucker assaulted me" said Mick.

"Well, did he now" replied the brother, before going to the bar and returning with an ice bucket full of thawed water. They exchanged glances and both men grinned."Bring out the gimp" said Mick.

"But the gimp's sleepin'" replied Ollie, tapping Percys head with his foot.

"Well, ah guess you're just gonna have to wake him up now, wont you?"

and Ollie tipped the bucket over onto Percys face.

By the time he got to his feet, Richards was soaked and struggling badly. He desperately gasped for breath, and his stinging eyes darted from Byrne to Byrne. He was having difficulty with what he saw.

"What in damnation are you too doing here" he blurted.

"We don't know" shouted mick "You're supposed to check the fucking place over before you lock up. Because of you, we didn't get home last night, and you know what that means, don't you. No one fed the fucking cat. Now Ollie, you get sweeping. I'll do the table tops, and you, you royal prick, you get the bar sorted. Thirsty men will come banging on your door soon and you'll be ready for them" and his voice deepened "By the way, PERCIVAL, the only people who get battered in there are the jailers, in case you haven't noticed the black eyes and the broken fucking teeth. Speaking of which, the next time you interrupt my bodily functions, I'll ram that cue so far up your fucking arse, that you'll be chalking it through your nose". The Byrne brothers got cleaning, and Percival Richards wondered where it all went wrong.

(vi)   ROOTS AND RAW DEALS

The lady at the Registrars reception desk was old and hard of hearing. When he said that he wanted to research the history of the Mulhares, dating back to the eighteenth and nineteenth centuries, she said that they kept very little information on hair, and certainly nothing relating to that period. She said that she could barely remember what her own hair was doing last time she checked.

"Old age will do that to you" she informed him.

When he shouted, it made little difference.

"THE MULHARES" he bellowed "THE MULHARES"

"Who cares?" she replied "Nobody, that's who. But you'll find out that for yourself, when you reach my age" and she became teary eyed before ambling off to the ladies to nurture her pride.

After rolling through the aisles for an hour or so, Bradford Shaw located a series of thick, well worn journals listed as 'Births, Marriages, Deaths And Brief Historys-Drumasheen/Meadowvale 1740 to 1850'. The earliest mention of his bloodline was in 1746, with the birth of Paraic Alfonsus St Francis Mulhare. The parents names were not clearly defined, but the words *'My boy, hung like a stallion, signed Dan'* were visible in old quill, and Bradford assumed that this was scribed by the proud father. Paraic Alfonsus, as he would sign himself, made a poor living as a *plague charmer*, and it was stated that he would play his tin whistle over an afflicted person, so as to coax the demon out, whereupon the said spirit could be treated to the onslaught of *'Shelelaghs and knobbed canes'*. One death too many, in 1792, and Paraic Alfonsus suffered a beating that he could not recover from, but not before siring three offspring, Liam Thomas Joseph Liam in 1772, Moses Abraham Adam Cain in 1773 and Teresa Doris Deborah Eileen in 1776.

It was written that Liam Thomas *'had tunes and rhymes for many a fete, but could stomach little drink'*. He took employment at the manor, and later married a stable boy named Jonathan. Teresa Doris joined a religious order and became a monk, but it was with Moses Mulhare that the lineage of Bradford Shaw really began. Moses, he learned, *came into the possession of a small plot of land by means of a duel involving but one pistol'*, basically Moses shot the owner and moved into his field. There he built himself a home, and took as his wife, Mary Margaret Mulhare. Paudie and Joseph were the resulting brood. Joseph left for foreign shores in 1794, shortly after his grandfathers death, and Bradford was able to trace the bloodline from there. Paudie *'provided great merriment and joy to the parish and was popular'*, before dying in suspicious circumstances in 1813. The land was sold at auction, and all that was stated in relation to it's whereabouts was *'laid out 'neath the Hump, where the bend of The Seanlaimh strokes the old oak tree'*.

It was almost noon and he had a lot to take in. He thought that this might be a good time to visit the tavern. He could relax over a drink and get to know the officers. It had been a long time since he sat in the company of the ranks. As he left the building, he was nearly knocked out of his chair by the gang of school boys that charged past, shouting and screaming. He roared after them, but they did not hear. They had other things on their minds. He ran down Quinlans Hill with the hounds of hell snapping at his heels. They were bigger boys, who could run faster and hit harder. He hurt easily and they knew it. He had held his lunch box tight to his chest, but they parted company as he rounded Devlins corner, so that he might pump his soft arms a little harder and gain a stride or two. His jam sandwiches and chocolate yogurt, spilled out onto the street, and he imagined that the gang would slip and slide and fall on their arses like the keystone cops, but they did not. They would have their pound of flesh, or in his case, several. What was the point? They would get him anyway. They always did. It would be over soon, he told himself, and he closed his eyes for a second to make that wish. Resting against the gable end of Hegartys, he watched them arrive. Wild. Rabid. Like a hunting pack.

They descended upon him, barking and growling. Spittle dripped from their open mouths, as they leaned on him, twisting his limbs and extracting that pitch of terror that was, after all, the game. They shouted orders amongst each other to hold him this way and that, and they tugged at his tee shirt till his belly lay on the cobblestone bed. He pleaded with them to stop, begged them, as they dragged large handfuls of sharp gravel across his back. His face was pressed into the ground, and a knee was planked across his neck to keep him in place. The pain was unbearable. They had lost control, baying at him, calling him 'a fat fuck' and threatening to rip him apart with their bare hands. He would die for sure, he thought, and he was only ten years old. He scrunched his eyes shut and screamed out for mercy. Then he heard an almighty crack. A vicious slap sent the biggest of them reeling headlong into the concrete pavement, followed by another and another. A deep voice, a mans voice, called out for action."Come on youse bastards, let's fuckin' have ya"

He could hear cries and footsteps as they took to the hills. A warm hand helped him to his feet and, without seeing his saviour, he embraced him wholeheartedly, and the floodgates opened.

He wanted to talk, but his tears wouldn't allow for it. That was okay. He was held and consoled, and when he was all cried out, he stood back and looked upon the face of the good Samaritan. It was a strange face. The complexion was fiery red, but did not appear to be sunburnt at all. The eyes were bloodshot, and sat unevenly above a swollen nose that displayed signs of injury around the nostrils. The ginger hair was cropped tight to the scalp, but did not show the wealth of grey that the weathered features would demand. For all that, though, it was a pleasant face, and when it spoke, the voice was soft and reassuring.

"And what's your name then, big man?

"Conor Mulcahy" said the boy "but the other kids all call me fats. And you?

"Derek Grady, but everyone calls me Doc" and he thought for a second " I don't think I like 'fats', so if it's all the one to you, I'll call you Conor, okay?"

Conor smiled. "That'd be great, Mr. Grady"

"Now..everyone calls me Doc, and that means you too, son"

Conors smile widened. Doc had called him son. If only his father would do that sometimes.

Derek Grady walked his new friend back to school. On the way, he learned that the boy was new to Meadowvale, and that he hated it. His father had been transferred to the town on a work contract, and Conor desperately missed his old boarding school mates. He had only recently turned ten, and he liked rice pudding. He could make a face in the folds of his stomach, and when no one was about, he set fire to his farts, which, of course, was hilarious to the two of them.

"So, what does your dad do, young man?" asked Doc.

"Well... I'm not really supposed to say" said Conor, and he whispered "He's a prison Chief officer"

Doc stared at Conor for traces of the bastard Chief. "Not Augustine, by any chance?"

Conor was confused. "Do you know him?" he said.

"Let's just say, we've met" and Doc whispered "I'm a warder too"

This caused great excitement with the lad. He saw Derek as a friend, now that he'd saved his life and all.

"Maybe you can come for tea" he said.

"Maybe not" said Doc "But you're a fine young man, and your father must be very proud of you"

Conor stopped smiling.

When he had spoken to the principle, and promised him a gangsters beating if Conor was ever bullied again, Doc left. On the way out, he spotted the boy re-enacting the saga to a group of amused looking kids.

"Good luck, son" he shouted.

"Good luck, Doc" said Conor "And thanks".

(vii)    THE EAGLE HAS LANDED

News of the beasts return had gone around the jail like wildfire. Shortly after noon, Prisoner Barry O Shea, reported to his cohorts on the Blue wing that, after overhearing a conversation amongst staff, Sean Talbot was, indeed, on his way. By 12.15pm, it was well and truly out, and a tension not felt in Meadowvale for many years, consumed the place. When officers attempted to lock up for lunch, there was trouble. Threats were made, and Officer Martin Clarke was punched and kicked as he attempted to remove a syringe. As staff responded, alarms went off elsewhere and four other jailers were injured trying to contain the situation. When the prison was finally secure, staff assembled in the circle. There was talk of riots and bodybags, and when Chief Mulcahy informed them that Talbot would be transferred out on Monday, and that all precautions would be taken to safeguard those working the weekend shift, they regarded his commitments lightly. The jail had been severely short staffed for years, and officers were forced to work on their days off to make up safe numbers. Even then, basic manning levels were not always met, and a very fine thread held the institution together. Therefore, the weekend shift meant everybody. They were not happy, but they took Augustine at his word and left for the tavern.

While they were gone, a prison van with tinted windows was admitted through the main gates of Meadowvale Place Of Detention. Flanked by six officers in riot gear, Sean 'The Beast' Talbot quietly made his way into the prison, and was added to her numbers. And so… it began.

(viii)    THE TURNING OF THE SCREW

Chief Officer Augustine Mulcahy, Garda Sergeant Peter O Driscoll and jail rat Ger Magner squeezed into the crime scene, and huddled over the toilet bowl. The object they stared at had come from at least three very different meals and, although no one mentioned it, each man wondered about the condition of it's previous owner. Should they need him for questioning, he'd be easily identified as the guy with the John Wayne gait. It stood to reason that some law must have been broken by it's presence, but, it played no part in their investigations and, after staring at it for a disturbingly long time, the bastard chief flushed it away.

The initial insults of 'THE CISTERNS OF CHARITY' and 'GER MAGNER SUCKS COCK' had been elaborated upon, and fresh graffiti adorned the phlegm stained walls of the officers restroom. 'THIS TILL IS CLOSED, GO TO NEXT CASHIER' was scrawled in large letters and an arrow pointed to the adjoining cubicle. 'SHITHOUSES FOR SALE- CONTACT GER THE KNOBGOBBLER' was posted for the amusement of the Meadowvale men.

"So... it's not here then" said O Driscoll and both men stared at him.

"It's not fucking here because Grady is pissing it against the wall as we speak" barked Magner "Get up to the tavern, and I'll guarantee you that prick is buying drink for the whole fucking town. Now, what exactly do you intend to do about that, Sherlock?"

Driscoll tapped at his chin. "Well" he said "If he is buying drink for the whole fucking town, Ger, I'd better get up there. After all, it's the least you owe me for having to listen to your bullshit." and Mulcahy had to separate them as they squared up to each other either side of the bog.

"But seriously" said Augustine "Ger does have a point. Grady stole that money and everybody knows it. Why don't you take him in and I'll make a call to the department to have him suspended. We both work in an environment where people need to be able to trust each other, Peter, and it's not fair on the other men. Let's not forget that some of those men are friends of yours too."

Peter O Driscoll was a man of integrity, and if Derek Grady stole that money, then, justice would be done, but until such time as that was established, he would not be swayed into action by a failed human being like Magner or by Mulcahy, whose rush to judgement seemed decidedly suspect to him. His response was deep south. He cocked his finger and winked.

"You boys ah might wanna stay grounded, ya hea" and he rolled imaginary tobacco on his tongue and spat "Aint gonna be no lynchin' till ah say so".

Back in his office, the chief sank into a recliner and swivelled. Things were going according to plan. He'd promised the big wigs, fresh scalps from Meadowvale, and Gradys was ready for presentation. The filthy drunk Grady. A man whose stay in the service had long outlived it's welcome. If O Driscoll didn't have the bottle, then Chief Officer Augustine Mulcahy would take the good doctor down, and all the fucking animals in Meadowvale would sit up and take notice. Who the man? He opened his locker and stared inside. £2000 in bank rolls stared back.

He'd only gone to the officers quarters that night to take a piss and, hey presto, opportunity knocks. Grady was out of it as usual, and when he discovered the cash, he knew it belonged to Magner. That dumb fuck counted his money out there every rent day, and still thought it was a secret. Mulcahy moved quickly. The graffiti was a bonus. He'd never done anything like that before... it was tremendous fun. Ger Magner sucks cock, nice one chief, a regular one of the lads. On the way out, he deliberately banged the exit doors so as to wake Grady, and he hid in the shadows to watch the drunk stumble off into the night. He'd cut it fine though. Only minutes later, Magner came past like Carl Lewis, and seconds after that, he was in tears. Grady was up shit creek without a paddle. Who would believe him. Christ, he probably didn't even know himself. Mulcahy locked away the evidence, and telephoned administration.

"I want a file put together on Derek Gradys sick record, including lates and management observations. Actually, open two. There's a few comments that I want to make myself"

The knife was in and he held the handle. Augustine was going to deliver. It should have felt so good, so why then did it feel so fucking bad.

(ix)    **RIGHT ON CUE**

Jailers work at the coalface. They are abused, beaten, bitten and worse. They work from dusk till dawn, and from sunrise to sunset. They are uneasy with the world and, sadly, they are very often nothing more than strangers to their families. While the good men and women of society watch their kids grow, share tender moments with their lovers, carve turkey at Christmas and live life to the best of their abilities, the warder goes toe to toe with the murderers, the rapists, the paedophiles, the junkies and the thieves. Most prisoners will tell you that the ultimate sentence is handed down to the Prison Officers, and the living conditions of the prisoner for the duration of his stint, is the working conditions of the staff for thirty years. Fifteen hour shifts in the shit and the piss and the blood and the puke, day after day, year after happy new fucking year, can harden you somewhat and the warder cares little whether the public are made aware of that or not. It's just fact.

In an ideal world, the department would insist on therapy, demand that *their* employees be given every opportunity to live normal lives, address the reality of the job... in an ideal world. In the world where the jailer lives, therapy comes cheap. It can be purchased in glasses in any tavern, or indeed, it can do house calls in the shape of bottles and cans from the off licence. And though it may not always be apparent, there is a peace that exists in the laughter and the bawdiness, in the revelry and the mayhem, much to the disgust of the Percival Richards in every jail town in Ireland and, I suspect, the world.

News of the Byrne brothers ordeal at the hands of the vicious publican had gotten round. Matty Morris and Phelim O Toole armed themselves with cues and took up strategic positions at the bar. As Percy dashed about dispensing therapy, they prodded his buttocks and poked his ribs, yelling at him to get a move on. Pablo Rogers stood silently at the counter, observing the exercise. His shirt was unbuttoned to the waist, and both Phidelma Gorry and Bridget Darcy ran their fingers across his chest and fondled his genitals. He raised his empty glass to Percy and nodded, but Percival was otherwise occupied and could not immediately oblige. As the proprietor attempted to fend off the advances of Morris and Devoy, a brandy glass came hurtling through the air and bounced off his head. Dazed and confused, he stared at Pablo.

"A fresh brandy in a clean glass, my good man" ordered Pablo "and whatever the lovely girls are having"

Phidelma and Bridget giggled childishly, took an earlobe each and groped with a little more passion. Tensions in the jail were at breaking point, and the craic was mighty.

Bradford Shaw was struggling with the oak doors when unseen hands whisked him through and down the steps that led into bar.

"There we go, horsey" said his huge assailant, before swaggering off in search alcohol. Bars like this were not unfamiliar to him. During his time in uniform, he'd blown many a storm and he understood the blood letting that went hand in hand with front line anxiety. By the time he'd reached the counter, he had been asked to go steady by several unsavoury looking characters to which he replied

"No, but I suppose a blowjob is out of the question"

He was feisty. The lads liked him. Percy wasn't quite sure why a man in a wheelchair would want to socialise in a pub where jailers toppled over as often as rainforest cedars, and the thought of another compensation case terrified him. Two brawling warders had landed on a disabled Spaniard in 1995, and the tavern paid out big time. Fearing a repeat performance, he asked Shaw if he wouldn't feel more comfortable in an establishment that catered for 'his kind'. Bradford was taught well in the field of diplomacy.

"My kind, sir, got our asses shot off, so that your kind could enjoy free enterprise in a free world. These hands haven't held a gun for far too long, but if I had one right now, I'd shoot you where you stand, you sonofa bitch"

There was a great cheer from the crowd, and Tony Ennis came charging across the room claiming that *he* had a gun, but that he fancied shooting 'the whore' himself.

"You owe our friend an apology, Percy" demanded Ennis.

Richards explained that he had never meant to offend anyone, and stated nervously that his family had it's own fair share of 'freaks'.

"I know" said Tony "I'm looking at one. You may not want to offer an apology, but, as sure as fuck you'll offer the man a drink. Make it that one" and he pointed at a bottle of Powers on the display shelf.

Percy sheepishly attempted to pour a measure for his new patron.

"Hi, Hi, what in the name a Christ are you at. The bottle, Percy" roared Ennis "Big fuck up, big stand down, that's the way it works. Now, hand me the bottle and don't have me come looking for it, or I *will* fucking shoot you".

Introductions were made all round, and each man shook Bradfords hand.

"You'll excuse me if I don't stand up gentlemen" he said "I'm breaking in new shoes, and they're a bitch"

Paddy Devoy was full of questions.

"Did you fight in Vietnam?" he asked.

"I was involved in that conflict, yes"

"And were you the guy that went into the jungle and formed your own cult" queried Paddy

"I think" said Bradford "that may have been Marlon Brando, you're thinking of".

"Maybe... you were the one who won all those Russian Roulette games then".

"No" said Bradford "That was Robert De Niro".

"I was shot myself" said Devoy, and he removed his trousers to reveal a star shaped wound to the right of his crack. "Tis fair nasty I'm told"

"Good Jesus" exclaimed Shaw "What conflict brought that about"

"Ah" smiled Paddy "twas only an altercation over a boundry wall with the neighbours, nothin' fancy like".

"Wasn't it a pity that you weren't hit an inch to the left" said Matty Morris, making reference to the proximity of the bullet hole to Paddys anus, "If you were, maybe you wouldn't be firing blanks", and everyone had a good laugh.

Bradford explained why he was in Meadowvale. He told them about the Mulhares, and explained that he had sourced a loose location for the family plot, by a tree that stood on the bend of the Seanlaimh, which he had desperate difficulty pronouncing.

The Seanlaimh, they informed him, was a river that ran the length of the county, and flowed just outside of the town, near the Dublin road. As for the tree, it could be one of many, unfortunately.

Pablo Rogers said that he had no intention of returning to work for the afternoon session and, that if Shaw was interested in making a day of it, they could have a few more pints and he'd be happy to take the General out to the Seanlaimh later. Bradford had settled in. He had not enjoyed himself as much since he had been with his own men. Sure. An afternoon in the pub with Rogers, as he would learn, was always an experience. But, first, he would have to return to the guesthouse to collect some things. He'd return shortly. On the way to Roches, he passed a large, sad looking lady pushing another tortured soul in a wheelchair.

"That poor bastard" thought Shaw "He looks worse than I do"

The General had no idea of the impact that Sean Hegarty was going to have on his future.

The after lunch shift went reasonably well. When there were no casualties following the 2pm unlock, staff got about their business as best as they could, keeping in mind that the presence of 'the beast' was always going to add an unwanted edge to the already rising tension in the jail. Much of the talk was of the Magner incident and rumour was rife. Doc had taken the money at gunpoint, knifepoint, he had beaten Magner with a shillelagh whilst wearing a bra, a pair of knickers, a thong and one popular story had a drunken Doc Grady sexually violate Magner with the shillelagh, whilst wearing a bra and a thong, and that he had taken Magners underpants as a trophy. The money, they surmised, had only been taken to help soften the blow for Doc when he sobered up and realised what he had done. Either way, he would be good for a few pints at the social club annual dance later that night.

(x)   **FRIENDS AND DEADLY DUOS**

Nora Hegarty was exhausted. She had pushed Sean for hours and he had become agitated and restless. He rocked and swayed, shaking the wheelchair, and she was having an awful time getting about. Several coaches had pulled into the town square, and she was expecting some new business from the arrivals. Normally, she would have spent the day preparing their accommodation and ensuring that there would be hot food available when they came knocking. But today was different. Today was all about Sean. Victor Roberts was a decent man, and he had been a help to her, but she couldn't expect him to dedicate himself to her on this occasion. Sean was her son and, as she stared at the manchild before her, she felt more love for him now than she had ever done. His need was greater than that of the hopefuls who searched for Jesus in the backwater towns of the pilgrimage trail, for they had something that Sean had lost a long time ago. They had hope. If God did not touch them on a leafy road outside of Meadowvale, then there was always Knock or Lourdes or some such place. Sean knew little of the world. Outside of his home and the potholed streets of Meadowvale, there was nothing, and if Christ is who you turn to when the darkness of this life consumes you, then she was that to her boy.

It hurt her terribly to see him like this, demented by his powerlessness, caged by his own form. She had wondered often if he was in there, hidden deep beneath the flailing limbs and the broken chatter. He had not spoken, as such, and there was a part of her that died when she understood that she would never again be called mother, but there moments when a stillness would fall upon him and a familiar expression would take hold of his face, like any second he might launch into the days events or break into song and whisk her away in a waltz, like he used to do, such a long, long time ago. But that expression would fade, always, and his eyes would drift away from her... and he was gone. She held his face in both hands and kissed his cheek, before heading for home.

Ger Magner sat nervously in the passenger seat of the car, and kept his eyes peeled. God forbid that anyone should ever find out what he was up to. He wanted to get this meeting over with as quickly as possible and his constant need to keep checking out the rear window meant that he didn't fully grasp what David Orr was saying. Orr handed him a series of tourist brochures and hospitality pamphlets, and outlined a business plan.

"If we choose our advertising carefully" he was saying "we can market the guesthouse to our target audience before and after they arrive. The place will need some refurbishing, of course, but if things go according to plan, you'll be able to pick it up for a steal and our total outlay won't cripple us"

Magner missed a fair bit of that. "Sorry, Dave, what were you saying?"

Orr reassured him. Everything was in hand. Provided Ger kept fabricating complaints against Hegarty, the bastard Orr could justify his recommendation for Seans compulsory removal to care. It would only be a matter of weeks before the old lady crumbled, and Magner would be on hand to relieve her of the unwanted pressures of the business. A reasonable offer would allow her the financial space to elevate her son from the squalor of basic residential accommodation. Hey presto, everyone's happy.

"But what if they check out the complaints" said Magner "All of the signatures are false, sure, didn't I sign the fucking things myself"

"They *have* been checked out, Ger" replied Orr "What the fuck do you think I've been doing here for the past month... Jesus man, get with the programme"

With that, there was an almighty wallop on the passenger window that had both men off their seats. Orr was horrified at the sight that stared in at them.

"What the hell is that" he screamed.

"That's Grady" shouted Magner and he dived for cover.

Doc tugged at the door handle and clawed at the window.

"COME OUT YOU FUCKING TRAMP, MAGNER" he roared "COME OUT TILL I BATE YA, YE LYIN' PIECE A SHIT"

Magner cowered and pleaded with Orr to drive. The car took off with a wheel spin and disappeared round the bend. They had travelled a mile or so before they pulled over. Ger was distraught. They had been seen together. The first crack had appeared. Orr calmed him down. There was nothing to worry about. So what, they'd been seen. The man was obviously a moron, a Neanderthal. Their association would mean nothing to him, why would it? But later, as Orr hit the motorway, something sat badly with him and he was concerned.

Bradford Shaw got the guided tour. A look behind the curtains of rural Ireland with Pablo Rogers as host. Just outside the town lived the Heffernans, who held prayer meetings every Monday and Wednesday, fireside ceilis on Tuesdays and Thursdays and no holds barred orgies on Fridays between 8pm and midnight. Podge Horan owned the local drapery, and once claimed that he had spent two weeks living in Graceland with the king, where, he maintained, he'd penned 'In the ghetto' for Elvis. Later it was revealed that he'd actually suffered from a bout of depression, and merely locked himself in the garden shed for the fortnight. His mother, God rest her, was seen leaving out plates of bacon and cabbage for him. When he came out of it, he had no recollection of the events, and Mrs. Horan, knowing his great love for rock n' roll, made up the story to Podges delight. No one ever had the heart to tell him and he had reworked the song several times since. Kathleen Murphy was the towns chemist, and she spent her evenings researching the effects of concoctions that she had prepared in her basement laboratory. She had invited Pablos collegue, Ian Harten, round for dinner one evening, and he recounted how she had jabbed something into the base if his skull as he spooned his way through a decidedly odd textured soup.

"There was a sensation of floating" he would tell the men later "and an unshakeable urge to flap my arms." He would describe the experience as "not unpleasant" and stated a desire to dine there again. Throughout the town, there were cross dressers, religious zealots, descendants of the little people, mutton barons and a myriad of strange and wonderful characters that made Shaw proud of his heritage.

The Seanlaimh lapped against the grassy banks of its route and sparkled beneath the last rays of the fading sun. A well worn path followed its course, and they found no difficulty in guiding the chair along the trail. The session in the tavern had made them giddy and laughter came easy. They discussed concubines and exotic places, trials and lost dreams. They were friends. Paul explained that the 'Pablo' tag had stemmed from his Mexican complexion, and Shaw agreed that there was, indeed, an Hispanic flavour to Rogers. Tall and lean, his jelly jarred hair gave him all the hallmarks of a South AmericanRhett Butler and it was apparent that frankly, he didn't give a damn. In contrast Bradford had been the all American boy in his day. Square jawed and crew cut, he would have been a fiercesome sight on the battlefield, and no matter how hard he tried to mask it, the sadness of his situation hung on his voice whenever he talked of the forces.

Pablo produced a hip flask and they rested. The view was breathtaking and both men agreed that Irish folklore was born of such sights. Tir Na Nog, Queen Maeve, Na Fianna and a thousand other tales were spawned from the mystic landscapes of the Gaelic countryside.

"I've heard some mad shit about the history of this place" said Pablo "Stories about dancing goats and crazy fucking highwaymen, not to mention the visions. Who knows, Bradford, maybe your ancestors were around to see it. This old river could tell a few tales. Seanlaimh is Irish for 'old hand' and it's been clawing away at the land around here for centuries". And they watched as it cascaded it's way into the distance, till it disappeared around a great bend.

"On a bend on the Seanlaimh" exclaimed Shaw "That's how the register described my folks property. This could be where the Mulhares lived. I hate to ask, Pablo, but would you mind pushing me just a little further".

The oak tree had grown black with age, and it leaned badly toward the river. Neither men could believe that it had lasted this long, and Rogers warned Shaw not to over excite himself.

"This could be any of a hundred trees along the banks of the river. You're talking about something that stood nearly two centuries ago."

But Bradford was sure. This was it. He just knew it and that was that. Paul scaled the old boundary wall that circled the field. He wandered off through the high grass and vanished over a hill. A few minutes later, he returned shaking his head.

"You wont fucking believe this, my friend" he said "but there's the ruins of a house in there, and by the looks of it, it dates back to the eighteen hundreds".

They made their way to the field gate, where Bradford caught his first look at the homestead. He was overcome.

"My people lived here" he said, and an uncharacteristic tremble floated on his voice "This is the first time I ever felt like I belonged to something other than the army, like it's a home, a base. I never really had that outside of barracks. My father was a soldier, and we grew up there you see"

A rusted sign hung from the gate. They hadn't noticed it before, in all the excitement, and it drew their attention. There was something scrawled in paint, faded, barely legible. Pablo cleaned away some caked mud that partially obscured the letters and he read.

"Ri..o Gra... nde. Fuck" he said "It's Rio Grande. This belongs to a jailer. I know the bastard. It's Ger Magners place".

Bradford Shaw was excited. "But he's one of you guys, isn't he"

"Oohh no sir, he is not." Said Pablo "Ger Magner is a filthy, horrible animal who just happens to work in the same job, don't make him one of us, no sir".

"I wouldn't mind meeting him though, if that's possible" said Shaw "I'd kinda like to talk to him about this place".

"Well that's settled then" grinned Rogers "We have our annual jail ball tonight, and you're coming as an honorary screw. The fuckpig will be there, you'll see him then. Now, get yer best frock on, Bradford. You'll be on everyones card for a dance".

Shaw held out his hand "Call me Brad, I insist"

Pablo Rogers and Brad Shaw ambled off in the direction of town singing Bruce Springsteens 'The River' as they went.

(xi)    MAN AND BOY

By the time Augustine Mulcahy arrived at the club, he was feeling guilty. Guilty on all fronts. He desperately wanted to show his son just how much he loved him, but genuinely didn't know how. *He* had never been shown and it wasn't something that he'd learned to master. As soon as he walked in from work, his wife told him what had happened. She had received a call from the school, to say that Conor had been involved in an incident and needed to go home, could someone please come and collect him. When she spoke with Principal O Dwyer, he informed her that Conor had been attacked by bullies, but that a prison officer from the jail, a Derek Grady, had intervened and that Conor had been saved from a, potentially, more serious assault. Apparently, Grady had outlined to the school authorities why it was in their best interests to prevent any recurrence of the situation, and O Dwyers hands were still shaking when Eileen arrived to collect her son. The boy had bruises and lacerations to his neck and stomach, but a G.P had seen to him and, of course, a full report of the incident had been made to the Gardai.

Mulcahy wanted to run to his son and embrace him, like he could somehow smother the awfulness away. He wanted to cry for him, cry with him, tell him that it would all go away, that daddy was going to make it better. But he could not do any of those things. Instead, he just stood there and stared blankly at an overweight child, who shuffled nervously beneath his glare. And when the boy had escaped the silence, to find solace in the tender arms of his mother, Mulcahy closed his eyes and remembered. Fat little Augustine, fat little calf. The cane, blood spraying from it as it cut through the air, the pleas for mercy, the pain, the torture, the cane, the cane, the fucking cane. He ripped his fathers photograph from the mantelpiece and smashed it against the wall. When Eileen and Conor rushed into the livingroom, they found him on his knees with tears streaming down his face... and he told them everything.

He recounted his experiences in unbearable detail, stopping from time to time to compose himself, but never actually allowing their consolations. It was, after all, his burden, and he'd carried it with him every second of every day for a lifetime. When he was through, he was exhausted. Though he knew that he was an innocent, he felt ashamed, weak in their eyes, and his first emotion was one of regret for having tainted their image of him somewhat. They, of course, saw things differently. Underneath that sometimes cold exterior, there was a hurted, confused little boy still screaming out to be saved, and it was Conor who reached out to him first. There had been an emotional wasteland that existed between them and Augustine had always been afraid to go there, afraid perhaps that he may stumble. But, that night, they had charged out of the trenches and into battlefield in search of each other. Like lost soldiers, they would lead each other home, but, as they limped closer in the blitz, a ringing broke the silence and stole the moment. Mulcahy was alone again, alone with them. The doorbell rang once more, and he left them, holding each other, sobbing.

He welcomed the babysitter and went upstairs. Eileen followed, and in the silence they got ready for the night ahead. The events of the past few days raced through his mind, and the guilt of his deception snarled at his conscience like a hungry beast. He had so desperately sought the approval of his peers, that he had allowed an insanity to take hold and he felt now that he had unravelled badly in the theft. And then there was the boy. History without the cane, he thought. He had so far to travel, but a traveller he would be. Things would change. *He* would change. Before they left, she completed the checks, dusted him down and fixed his collar.

"He loves you" she said.

"I know that" he replied.

"And you love him"

"I know that too" he said and his words were calming to him, like he had taken the first steps back.

"He misses you when you're not here" she said "Why don't you bring him with you on Sunday, just for an hour. Spend some time together. You need that too".

He nodded and they left.

Now they were here, and he thought of Conor and Eileen, of Doc and the money, of Talbot and the men and of just how much he hated fancy dress. Sister Augustine of the sacred heart and Father Eileen of St. Michaels drifted into the crowd, where he wondered how he had allowed things to get so fucked up.

(xii)    A NIGHT TO REMEMBER

Matty Morris had corset rash, which surprised him. It wasn't like he hadn't ever worn one before, of course he had, but this one irritated him, and he had to fumble through his petticoat to rip at the itch.

"Cheap aul' shite" he thought "I shoulda worn one o' the others".

But, if he was to the queen, he would have to maintain his decorum. So, he only scratched his belly when he had to, and he only tugged at his crotch when it was absolutely necessary. After all, she *was* royalty. Clint Eastwood glared at the ample breasts of Phidelma Gorry as they almost popped from the bodice of Marie Antoinette. Matty thought that he was a dirty swine.

"FILTHY PIG" he shouted, and Clint swaggered over.

"I saw you Rogers" said her majesty "You're a dirty ting".

"And you might look like Norman Bates with a tiara, Matty" replied Clint "but I'm a gonna ride you like a rodeo buck… YEEHAW!", and he grabbed at the regal gown.

Queenie raced through the crowd laughing hysterically with the cowboy in hot pursuit.

Charlie Chaplins and cat skinned cavemen staggered about spilling ale, and at least two vampires urinated in flowerpots. Paddy Devoy presented himself as The Furhrer, and sported a red bubble nose.

"I'm Rudolph Hitler" he announced, and no one could ever have imagined that the nazi ever downed so much whiskey. Paddy had served with the Irish forces overseas and, somewhere along the way he had gone quite mad. He once claimed that The Battle Of Little Big Horn had actually taken place in the Loire Valley in 1943, between advancing German troops and a crack team of Sioux and Apache Indians, recruited by the allies.

"You see" said Paddy "the jerries had no answer for the poisoned darts" and he pointed to an evil looking pimple on his neck to indicate that he had fallen foul of "dem injuns" in the Autumn of 1944… ten years before he was born. Paddy was great craic, and he marched around the hall S.S style, occasionally breaking into a jig to the applause of the men.

Doc Grady went to the bar and called for coffee, black. He had come as himself, and when Leopold Bloom a.k.a Leonard Fennell asked him who he was supposed to be, he answered that he was a recovering alcoholic and, that the coffee was just a prop. He found the darkest corner of the hall and faded into the shadows. He didn't want to answer any questions that weren't asked of himself, and he would be busy enough with those. He closed his eyes and rested.

It was 1995 and, after months of travelling to and from Liverpool, Jean had agreed to visit Meadowvale. She was still doing shifts at The Love Nest, but only now and then. She was fiercely independent and would accept no financial help from him. Her profession bothered him as much as his bothered her, but she was the strongest person he had ever known and she knew her own mind.

She was welcomed by all and, when she left two weeks later, they were well and truly smitten. There were tears at the station, followed by a phonecall a day. They could talk. Christ, could they talk. Whole evenings would see them lost in conversation and they pretty much knew everything they needed to know. One evening, as she prepared a client for 'The Knee Trembler', she just got up, dressed and left. Four hours later she was in Meadowvale, and by the end of the year, she was Jean Cooke Grady. They were happy, and that should have been that.

Alas, it was too good to last,
a heart does not control such things,
a single Magpie took to flight,
and she was swept away upon it's wings.

By May of 1997, she was waking up to find him screaming Francis Hogans name into the dark, and shouting at him to get the fuck out of their house, or their bedroom, or their bed. He was drinking heavily again, and they didn't talk so much anymore. She did what she could. She dragged him from pubs, cleaned him, nursed him, talked him down and built him up. Lover, soul mate, friend. But none of it was enough and, when she found *herself* starting to soften, to surrender to *his* ways, she made the decision. She would die for Derek, but she would not die with him. It was time to fly. Bye, bye blackbird. He sipped his coffee, closed his eyes again and enjoyed the good times.

Dinny O Brien stood outside the entrance to the hall, and murdered a cigarette. He was nervous. Jim Gilmore held a place of great respect in the hearts of the boys and girls of Meadowvale Jail, and tonight, Denis was going to make it known to all that he was he was an item with big Jims widow. Now... how would that go down? Veronica tugged at his arm to get a move on. She was aware of his concerns, but she was aware, also, that Dinny O Brien was a living legend throughout the service. He had been a tutor to the trade, and there was not a decent officer in the system who spoke of him without regard. "Come on" she said "we're missing the craic"

"I'll be along in a second" said Dinny "Shur, you go ahead"

"No" said Veronica "*We* go ahead".

And they did.

Bradford Shaw had collided with the table before he even knew he'd been rolling. The beer had gone to his head and, for all intents and purposes, he was a drunk driver. He made his apologies to a gentleman that he seemed to have woken up.

"Christ guy" he said in his southern drawl "this baby's outta control".

Doc was impressed with the prop.

"How in the fuck did you come across that?" he asked.

"Bought it in Michigan" said Shaw.

"Well… I have to admire your commitment" said Doc, who was trying to put a name to his new friend "I just hope you get invited to a lot of these affairs. I'm going to the bar, fancy a drink?"

"Yes" said Bradford "I most certainly do".

The band called for singers, and Matty took to the stage, with the twins for backup. They cranked out a version of the old Ink Spots classic 'Whispering Grass', which lead nicely into the slow set. Doc had spotted Dinny slipping in with Veronica, and he knew that the big guy was concerned about the night ahead. They had been confidants and, although everybody in the room was aware of Dinnys relationship with Veronica and was delighted for them, Doc was the only person that was 'officially' in on the secret. Denis had told him once, that the most poignant memory he had of his parents was watching them take to the floor in a Nashville marquee. He was a child then, and the experience of America would have left its mark anyway, but seeing them that night, so in love, so… happy, would remain with him for all his days.

"It was the first time that I realised that they were people" he'd say "and not just my parents"

Bradford was in deep conversation, when Doc asked him to hold the thought. He went to the stage and had a word with the musicians. He took the microphone and asked for the dance floor to be cleared. In an emotional address, he talked of the good days, of friends past and present, and he paid tribute to their comradery and support in the face of adversity.

"There are great men" he said "and then there are great jailers. There are women who ease the pains of broken men and then there are angels who lay their hands on shattered spirits. Ladies and gentlemen... I give you Dinny and Veronica" and the band launched into 'The Tennessee Waltz'.

They floated. His riverboat gambler, her plantation belle. Dignified. Graceful. Proud. It was reverence more than silence that descended on the others. There were memories and knowing glances shared, but no one broke the moment, and it was a testament to the occasion that a licensed premises full of prison officers should maintain a hush in honour of another. Jim would have been pleased. When the final notes were played, the applause rattled the tiles and there were shouts of "GO ON YE GOOD THING" and "OATS FOR THE HORSE". Normality had been restored. Pablo raced through the crowd pushing Bradford in a wheelie, Matty lifted his royal skirt and can canned without his underpants and all around husbands and wives, jail lovers and drunken flings line danced and be bopped till the early hours. It was *their* world, *their* domain and they fucked the begrudgers.

To their employers, they were rabble, whose very existence cast a shadow over the Darwinian theory, but what did they know. The pencil pushers of the Dept. had never witnessed the blue monster. The sight of them, all charging in unison at some jail upheaval was awesome, and they were the human embodiment of a solar eclipse to the weapon wielding inmates of their attention. The evolution of the warder had taken place on the underbelly of society, and they were what they were only because they had to be.

(xiii)   **TALBOT**

Tadhg Sheridan worked the night shift. He told the lads that he did so to avoid having to sleep with the wife, but, if truth be known, the place had stripped him over the years and he just couldn't face it during the day. He patrolled the segregation unit in between crosswords, and the only entry to his night guard report concerned the prisoner in cell 7.

*"Prisoner Sean Talbot sat awake throughout the shift. Did not require assistance"*.

Harmless enough... or so it seemed. But 'The Beast' Talbot had not been harmless for a very long time if, indeed, he ever had been.

It had been a difficult birth. He had been a difficult child, and lengthy spells in juvenile had not dulled his zest for destruction at all. There were times when his mother had regretted ever surviving the labour and his father, a drunken layabout, grew tired of buckle whipping *'the bastard'* , and went to the bookies to avoid his company. At eighteen, he took a bullet in the leg for assaulting the wife of a known provisional, and later served 6 months in the big boys jail for the same offence. He enjoyed only moments of freedom over the next 10 years, and notched up a litany of convictions for burglary, car theft, possession of narcotics, fire arms and he served time for his role in a botched bank raid in which a Garda was seriously injured. He discovered heroin sometime in the late Eighties and he was diagnosed HIV positive in 1990. But, it was in 1991, when he crawled from the cesspit of Dublin street crime and became a creature, an abhorration... the beast.

He was out on temporary release, parole if you wish, after serving six months of a two and a half year sentence for larceny. There had been a major seizure atDublin Port and, although the usual suspects had some supply of smack, the price had gone through the roof. Dirtbird economics is a fickle thing, and the junkie is a desperate animal at the best of times, but, when things get down and dirty, the fuckers would skin your hide for a fix, and Talbot was more desperate than most. There had not been a problem in the nick. Maybe you'd have to suck some dick, or take one in the ass, but it was a small price to pay for the hit. This shit stank.

He recalled in court that she looked young, no more than 27 or 28. The barrister told him later that she had given birth to her second child only two weeks earlier. He hadn't even noticed the stitches. When they burst in a mish mash of blood and screams and wails, he had thought that he was *"a bona fide love machine, a regular fucking Valentino"*. He recounted how the older child, the eight years old, *"Shiela or Shauna or some bitches name"*, had interrupted him before he had a chance to *"finish the job"*. She had torn into his buttocks with her nails and she had smashed a lamp across his skull. He told the trial judge that he *"got an infection in the arse from her glitter polish"* and that he *"would have stuck a tail in her too, but the baby woke up, and the whole thing got dodgy"*. In his defence, the barrister said that Mr. Talbot had never meant to rape anyone, and that he had broken into the house merely in search of drug money. He said that his client was *"delirious from the ravages of his addiction"* and asked that his condition be taken into consideration upon sentencing. But the judge had heard enough. Talbot had not even attempted to mask his depravity in court, and it had been unsettling for all those who were present during his testimony. He was sentenced to 12 years without leave to appeal.

The papers labelled him 'The Beast' and it stuck. He made sure of it. He became a threat to everyone, the officers, the medics, the prisoners and, a year into his sentence, he was one of the only sex offenders in the system that freely associated with the mainstream scum of the prison population. Six months later he called the shots, and he put their loyalty to the test on the rooftops of Meadowvale Jail one unforgettable day in 1993. But, of all the expressions that he had invoked in his life, the look on her face when he climbed in through the nursery window, took the biscuit. He leaned back on his jail bunk and masturbated furiously, not caring that Tadhg Sheridan might see.

# CHAPTER THREE : SATURDAY

(i)          BREAKING THE WAVES

Saturday was one hot day. Officers and prisoners sweltered in the morning haze, and long before noon, tempers were frayed. The sun is no good for the jail. It heightens the claustrophobia of the place, adds an edge to the inmates, makes them resentful. The usual banter that existed between lags and warders was in short supply. A line was drawn, it appeared, and you stood on one side or the other, like it or not. By lunchtime, some prisoners had made it clear that they did not want to be unlocked for the afternoon, and this was a worrying sign for the staff. Not all prisoners are bad, and these individuals had decided that they did not want to be involved in anything that may be about to happen. Talbots influence was striking. He still hadn't been moved out of segregation, and already the place was on a war footing. Tensions had been rising in Meadowvale for quite some time, but the beasts return had accelerated the descent and inmates that had previously been classed as disruptive, were now becoming downright disturbed. He was their David Koresh, their Jim Jones, their divine intervention. Inmates who had never actually met Talbot, told newcomers of his power, of his struggle, of his steely resolve at the helm of the revolution, and it did not go unnoticed by the jailers that there was never a mention of his depravity or his savagery or his need to… just… fucking… destroy. The staff had put pressure on the union to have him transferred **A.S.A.P**, the union went to management and the management took it to the governor. Phone calls were made, but to no avail. First thing on Monday, he would be gone, bottom line.

Fall in for prisoners is normally a chaotic affair. In the throng of five hundred men descending on the kitchens, drugs and porn mags exchange hands, and messages are shouted from one side of the house to the other. But today, an eerie silence shrouded the operation. Convicts huddled in whispers, eyeballing the staff, challenging their approaches. There was a sense of some epic confrontation in the making, something so sinister and surreal that the natural instinct of decency is to ask why. But, to the guardians of the gaol, this *was* the job, and they were no strangers to the tragedy that came with it. The wings were emptied remarkably early and the staff were in the tavern long before they would have liked… a shocking statement to make.

The fancy dress festivities had gone on till some ungodly hour and the men were rough in its wake. Trembling hands steadied on cold pint glasses, and stout heads and lager froths decorated the floor from the bar to the tables where they gathered.

Doc Gradys hands shivered more than most, and his coffee shot from the cup in all directions but, to his credit, he was holding tough. He had been some boy in his day. He had led the charge to the tavern, breakfast, dinner and tea for almost an eternity and, long before big Peter O Driscoll had unlocked him to slop out, he had known all about the rot. It had been a lonely voyage, and though he could not recall the hour or the year when it happened, he had grown old somewhere along the way, and the reflection that he caught on restroom mirrors and pub front windows was lined and cracked and beaten up. But, cold sweats and shakes or not, Doc Grady was fighting back.

Paddy Devoy couldn't keep his head still. When he tried to hold it up, it took on a life of it's own and it bobbed and weaved and nodded uncontrollably. When he relaxed it, it slumped against his chest and he stared at the others past a brow that was far too pasty and swollen for any Homo Sapien creature. Phelim O Toole was having his own problems, but he thought that if he stayed talking to Paddy, nature would take its course and Jailer Recovery Syndrome would kick in.

"So… you alright there, Patrick?" he said to the back of Devoys head.

"No" mumbled Paddy in obvious distress.

"Shur, you'll be grand" said Phelim "Have a few small ones and you'll be steppin' out with Sean Hegarty by tea time".

There was no response.

"Patrick?"

Still no response.

"Pat?" shouted Phelim, and he pulled Devoy by the shoulders till his head rolled back with its mouth agape and rested against O Toole. Phelim managed to get an arm around him, and he moved in for a closer inspection. The teeth, all ten of them, had the appearance of aged ivory and past them, great globules of mucus were in conflict for the right to steal past a dangerously enlarged epiglottis. The eyes were only part alive and were glazed, giving Paddy the appearance of a lobotomy recipient.

"Fuck me" said Phelim "the whore's dead".

"Shake him" demanded Doc "Make him undead"

Devoy was trying to get his bearings as best he could. He was warm and comfortable, and this meant that he was most probably in his own bed. The bristles on the arm across his neck, combined with the manner in which his name was being hollered surely meant that the wife was upon him.

"Think, Paddy, Think"

Phelim was getting genuinely concerned, when he saw Devoys lips begin to move.

"Thank Christ" said O Toole, and he leaned in just in time to hear the words "I love you, sweetie" before Devoy kissed him on the lips.

Paddy would later say that he only realised it wasn't his wife he had been kissing, when the punch in the face brought him around.

"Mildred" he said "punched much harder".

Laughter came easy that lunchtime, and the stress of their situation lifted a little with every jibe and joke and insane act… but it would return. It always does.

(ii)   HE AINT HEAVY

Harsh winds of despair blew through the Liverpool of the 1960s. Unemployment was rife and, long before the Beatles put The Cavern on the map, scousers had little to sing and dance about. Factories folded overnight, and despite the best efforts of the Labour movement, whole communities found themselves on the breadline. Families lived hand to mouth and anything of worth ended up on the pawnbrokers shelf. It was the age of the wheeler dealer, of the rag and bone man, of the buy cheap – sell quick tip your hat man, and it was the time of Henry Cooke. Henry Cooke, trinket trader, carpetbagger, father, sadly missed by his only child. Jean remembered crying by her window, as he leaned into a winter wind at 5.30am on a market morning. He would wave, always, to reassure her and, at some ungodly hour, he would shuffle in, with his collar about his face to hide the sores and blisters from the ravages of the season.

In the weeks leading up to Yuletide, he would raid a sparsely filled closet, and his Sunday best would be ironed and folded, and exchanged for the brokers ticket. But Father Christmas always remembered her. Dolls and prams that had passed through the trembling hands of more than one child, delighted *her*, and she was never embarrassed when kids gathered in the street to survey the spoils. Never embarrassed, but so often sad. She would be aware of him, watching her from the front porch, in his scuffed shoes and his badly patched clothes, and though his smiles never said, she knew of his sacrifice. Henry was a good man and she loved the bones of him. Whenever they could, they went to Anfield, where she was held higher than the titles and the medals and the cups, and the golden boys of the Shankly era adorned her wall long after it was fashionable for them to do so. She was a happy child, who never knew if they were rich or poor or frowned upon. They just were. He instilled in her an independence and a pride that no one could take from her, a never say die attitude that would carry her when friends and lovers did not. But that fabric would be stretched, and when the cancer grabbed hold of him and sucked his life away, their fight meant nothing. It stripped him of his flesh and his dignity and his faith, and, for he had always been such a proud man, it was a shame to watch. In those final days he lay with them, helpless in his suffering and, when the words were gone, she stroked his hair and kissed his cheek, while he battled and fought and lost. When he passed he was loved, admired and fondly remembered, and if we are honest, truly honest, that's the best that any of us could hope for.

She was alone for the first time. She had only the loss, the loss of hope, the loss of self, the loss of knowing absolutely that somebody, somewhere believed in her when the world in its fury did not. She drifted a little at first. Rather than embark on the road that he had paved for her, she took a different course, easier, lonelier... darker, and when she had learned to accept it, she drifted a lot. Men wandered in and out of her life. Some beat her, some did not. Some took from her what they could, others gave a little in return and she became numbed to it, rolled with it, worked with it. Jean Cooke, provider of fantasies in happy half hours. They could have what they wanted, but not from Henrys little lass. No, they could buy their pleasures from the lovely Maxine, mistress, madam or just plain whore, the price was the same. They moaned, groaned, squealed, grunted, farted and cried, but they paid, she lived... just about. She was never aware of them. They were out there, outside the windows of her soul, never seeing, never searching. And then one day, one ordinary day, she stared through the windows of another and saw the horrible, terrible sadness that life had punched into the soul of Doc Grady... and she was not alone anymore.

She knew them, of course, knew them well. She had seen them a thousand times. Every time she passed a mirror or caught her reflection on the shop fronts of stores that she could not afford to browse in. They were in there with her, barking back at the world, these Meadowvale men all battered and broken. They recognised her too. They saw the scars and never had to ask. They just unlocked the door and welcomed her in like a friend from the cold. And she remembered crying at her window, as Doc leaned into a winters wind on an early shift. He would give a thumbs up, always, to reassure her and, at some ungodly hour, he would shuffle in with his mask up, to hide the wounds and demons of his trade. Jean Cooke was home. Which made it all the harder when the cancer got to him too. Not the cancer that feeds off the organs or strips the bones, but the parasite that devours the spirit, the pestilence of the prison, the plague that had Derek Grady good and proper. She had lived through it before, barely. This time she could not take the gamble. She took her things and left.

Saturday was one hot day, and she was glad to be off. The café would be busy with tourists and shoppers, and the city would be alive with the hustle and bustle of the weekends activities. She couldn't handle it today. She'd had a rough night. She dreamed that she was on a ship at sea. A great storm raged, and when she looked out from her cabin, she saw that a small boat was being towed behind. In the boat, Henry Cooke and Derek Grady screamed and waved their arms, but no one came to their rescue. She ran to the deck and tried to reel them in, but the rope snapped and a huge wave took them into the night, as she sailed away. She had woken at 5.30 am and couldn't get back to sleep. She was tired now and, as the sun poured over her face, her eyes became heavy. She lay on the sofa, and just as she began to fade, the phone rang. She struggled to her feet and answered it. The voice that came back was Dinny O Briens.

(iii)   **IF YOU GO INTO THE WOODS TODAY...**

Victor Roberts spent the morning with them. It had been tough. Sean had been restless since the early hours, and when they had tried to administer his daily shot, he had reacted angrily. The routine was familiar to him by now and the sight of the needle caused him to lash out, striking Nora about the chest and knocking her over. But it was the look of disbelief, that expression of disappointment, like she had somehow... abandoned him, that had hurt her the most. And when she lay across him, grappling to restrain him, there was that moment when he stared through her, as if he hated her for what she had done, for what she had taken. She burst into tears and ran down the hall.

Victor sat at the kitchen table, exhausted. They sipped their tea in silence and listened to him rocking the wheelchair in the next room. When the first guests arrived on her doorstep, they were greeted by a tired, bleary eyed old woman, who struggled to communicate with them over wails and groans that echoed throughout the house. They made their excuses and left.

"I can't do it" she told Victor, sobbing "I'm not able anymore. Maybe David Orr was right. Maybe Sean would be better looked after by the nurses and the doctors" and she imagined him standing by a hospital window... *lost... alone... adrift,* "And then again" she said "maybe not".

Victor put his jacket on. "I'll take him out for a while" he said "Get some fresh air. Would you like to come along?"

"That *would* be nice, yes,... I'll get my coat"

They shuffled off, unsure of their motivations, uncertain of their intentions and unaware that they were being watched.

When he walked in, he was shaking. Some of the faces were familiar to him, others not so. They had done damage together at some stage, no doubt, and though he could not produce a name, pleasantries were exchanged, and he moved on. Freshly brewed tea and neatly cut sandwiches were on offer but his stomach advised against it. He was nervous. There were pockets of conversation that might have interested him, had he been more confident, but he wasn't, so he edged his way past, apologising for any interruption he may have caused in doing so. Several rows of old school chairs formed a centrepiece and, as soon as things were underway, he slipped into the back row and sat reverently in the shadows. A heavyset man with a well trodden face addressed them and, once the top table participants were introduced, it was noted that a new member was amongst them. There was suggestion that he might like to share his burden, on the understanding, of course, that there was no obligation for him to do so. But he had come to them with his honesty and his desperation, and, struggling for composure, he leaned out from the gloom and spoke.

"My name is Doc" he said, trembling "and I'm an alcoholic". They welcomed him without question.

The ruin was just that. Sun bleached stones that had once seen the flicker of an open hearth fire, were scattered like dry leaves, and the formations that stood in the high grass bore only a passing resemblance to a home. It looked, for all the world, as if some great foot had trodden upon it, and Bradford Shaw would have been excused if he had seen it as just another dead thing. But he did not. He believed it had history, and it had. Moses Mulhare had killed for this land, although he would swear blind that his victim had taken a massive heart attack before the bullet ever struck him. Paudie Mulhare was conceived and born here. In a drunken passion, Moses had forgotten to wear his rosary beads to bed and he would later say that it was the absence of Christ that night that allowed his *"bastard seed to plant in de wife"*. Seanie Maguire was here. He would regularly visit with his lady friend, and it was always a source of great excitement and entertainment when Seanie took his lover into the spare room to fornicate. For a man whose vocabulary was limited at the best of times, he would assume the voice of an angel during intercourse and, for the duration of the exercise at least, the house would be filled with glorious hymns from the Latin mass. It brought tears to many an eye.

They felt that it was a credit to Seanies vocal chords that he had netted a lady of such high standing and, that she later turned out to be the transvestite son of Lord Richards, took nothing from the fact that Seanie Maguire had once courted the gentry.

The house had been witness, also, to the romances in Paudies life. Widely respected for his quickstep, he was not short of female admirers and, on any given ceili night, local women would sup on their stouts and permit their eyes the pleasure of his person. But it was the Widow Mac who caught *his* eye and it was common knowledge that they shared an intimacy from time to time, although she had always expressed a concern regarding Paudies relationship with the livestock that he shared his premises with. He was a father figure to them, he would tell her, nothing more than a shoulder to cry on. But, when she was gone, he told them the same thing of her. Paudies death took place in this house. For weeks after his demise, locals searched the place high and low, looking for the secret recipe, but it was not found. He'd hid his treasure somewhere safe and, now, he would not be available for comment. These stones saw the famine, the bloodshed of independence, the faces of the ages. Some of them were trampled underfoot by work horses, only to be thrown up decades later by tractors and combines. Yes, the ruin was filled with history... Bradfords history, and, as he stood there soaking up its atmosphere, he sensed that it could also be filled with his future.

How could this have happened. Two days ago, everything was going swimmingly. Now, because of one small incident, things were on a knife edge. David Orr shook his head. When the gorilla tried to bash his windscreen in, he had not been worried. They did not know each other and, as Magner was the focus of his anger, the brute may not have even noticed him in the car. Certainly, he would have seen no connection between them. But, for all that, David Orr was uneasy. Magner had become increasingly apprehensive, and his fear was that Gerards nerves would get the better of him and things would go belly up. So, David Orr found himself, this Saturday afternoon, skulking around Meadowvale, watching Victor and Nora, as they struggled to push Sean up the main street of the town.

"Clever bastards" he whispered to himself, as he worked out what the wheelchair was for. He should have gone into business with them instead of that incompetent fucker, Magner. Just his luck to have a cousin like Ger, and worse luck again to have ever met the bastard. It had seemed like such a good plan at the time. Well… anyway, he was here to do a job, and he may as well get it over with. Roberts was a *big, big* man, and he knew that the punch was going to hurt, but having Victor out of the picture would see the old lady all alone, and that would seal it for sure. He stepped out of his car and approached them.

Meadowvale was such a little place. If you were to stand on main street, you could, probably, bump into everyone you knew in an hour or so. Doc Grady did just that. The meeting had gone well enough. His head was still wrecked, but, at least, he wasn't alone. He had met the lads on their way back to work, and they had briefed him on the mornings events. The jail was as high as a kite. The prisoners seemed organised, almost ready for war. Talbot was low key and still in segregation. Mulcahy had promised to have him moved on Monday, but they were sceptical. The usual banter was missing and Doc could sense a tension in them that was tragically familiar. Shortly after they had gone, Bradford Shaw rolled by. Fresh grass clung to the spokes and dried mud caked the rims of his wheels. The exertions of manoeuvring his way through the countryside had left him exhausted, and he was glad of the opportunity to rest a while with Derek.

They talked of the previous nights excess, and Doc understood, for the first time in many years, what it felt like not to wake up as the butt end of everybodys conversation. Bradford was disappointed that he had not met with some guy called Magner, as he had hoped to discuss Rio Grande. He explained his situation to Grady. This very morning he had felt the power of his own heritage, and he was overwhelmed by it. There was to be a prayer meeting on the Holy Road this coming Monday, and he was due to fly back to the States on Tuesday. He was very much at the crossroads. America held nothing for him now. On his return, he would catch a taxi to his apartment, where he would unpack and take up his position by the window. He couldn't say for sure when or why he would leave that spot, only to relieve himself and order pizza. This had been the greatest experience of his life. He was more alive here than he had been since the shooting. Last night he had laughed and danced and sang songs. He'd been drunk and foolish in a way that... well... in a way that made him whole again. If this Magner guy was half decent in his business dealings, then who knows what road he might take. Doc was in the middle of explaining why the words decency and Magner rarely appeared together, when he took off down the street like a bull.

Sean Hegarty was a mess. His face was smeared with chocolate and ice cream had dripped into his pullover. Nora was daubing a cloth over him, when she was startled by an unwelcome voice. It was Orr.

"I was in the area, Mrs Hegarty," he said grinning "when I noticed you were out for a stroll. I see the poor creature's had a mishap, God love him. Well, any update?"

"Fuck off" she said "and keep moving"

He looked offended.

"Now, now, Mrs Hegarty, there's no call for that. After all, I'm not the one keeping this poor devil from the kind of treatment that he deserves"

Victor Roberts towered over him, and Orr wondered if there were any small men in Meadowvale.

"You heard the lady" barked Victor "Move along and there won't be any trouble"

"Now who mentioned trouble. We're all concerned about this mans future" and he stared at Sean, who was becoming increasingly agitated by his presence.

"You unfortunate bastard" said Orr, and he attempted to run his finger along the horrible scar that decorated the width of Seans skull. Victor would have hit him for sure. He would have hit him and Orr would have had him lifted for assault. But he never got that chance. Before David Orr had even made contact with Seans hurted face, he was sent reeling backwards by the sheer force of the abuse.

"WHERE IS HE, WHERE'S THAT LYIN' BASTARD HIDIN' HIMSELF"

Doc Grady was one angry man. Whatever Magner had done to him, David Orr wanted nothing to do with it. He turned on his heels and fled. They stood in silence and watched his tail lights disappear.

When the fucker Orr was well and truly gone, every one calmed down a little. Nora was shocked. How did Doc know a shitebag like that, and why so angry? Derek asked the same questions, and, noticing Seans predicament, what was the idea of the wheelchair. They traded tales and agreed to meet up later in the tavern. Now, Ger Magner had a posse on his tail.

(iv)    **POWDERKEG**

Dinny O Brien was trawling through his locker. Tomorrow would be his last day, and it would mark the end of an era, not just for himself, but for the prison service in Ireland. It was hard to believe, thirty years over, just like that. He sifted through the photographs and the memories that he had neatly parcelled, and there were cards from Christmases and birthdays that he had shared with the lads. One mans whole lifetime wrapped in a locker. Hard to believe, for sure.

There was a snap of Matty Morris on his wedding day, tall and proud, standing beside herself. They had insisted on Dinny posing for the shot. As best man he couldn't really refuse, and there he was, fresher then, younger I suppose. Such a pity that things hadn't worked out for them. They were happy, then things changed. They changed. The job will do that. Sad though. There was one of Dinny and Paddy Devoy, stepping out together on the dance floor at the Glentawn Strawberry Fair. That would have been about 1975 or 6, and Paddy looked just as mad back then. The locals were not impressed. Two big burly warders waltzing in plain view of the children, but they had some weekend, one of the great ones. There were photos of Mick and Ollie, Phelim, Tony, pablo and one of Bridget and Phidelma trying to pull down his trousers during the celebration mass that would usher in 1990. Doc had taken most of them. Before they lost him, Derek had been a fine amateur snapsmith, and indeed, he had remained a close friend to Dinny, even through the dark days of his descent. But, the image that cut him most was that of big Jim Gilmore. They were preparing to embark on their careers in the prisons, that last day of training, when someone caught the moment, and there it was. They were handsome chaps back then, October 13th 1967, and they believed that thirty years to the day, they would run from the service and challenge the world. But Jim had fallen along the way and Dinny had grown old. The world would be safe just a little longer. He closed his eyes and held the picture to his brow.

It was August 22$^{nd}$ 1993. The prisoners had smashed their way onto the roof, and the whole place was in chaos. Officers ran in all directions and the explosion of sound was deafening. Shards of slate were raining down from above, and bloodied faces appeared and disappeared, screaming as they went. Derek Grady was heading a team to the ladders, and they were suited up for action. They would have been the fourth such convoy to the front, and they needed an anchor man with experience. No one was as well versed in the art of combat as Dinny was in 1993. He had been a training instructor for years and he was the obvious candidate. But, even then, Dinnys past had a nasty habit of catching up with him, and events from another age had plagued him for weeks, and he had found himself drunk that day. He would regret it, of course, but he had no way of knowing that things would have panned out like they did. He was about to make his way, unsteadily, to the top, when Jim Gilmore appeared, all armoured up, and replaced him. Jim told the Chief of the day that Dinny had injured his back playing football, and that it would be better all round if he took the anchor. As he left, he laid his great hand on Dinnys shoulder.

"For a friend, Dinny" he said "For a friend"

That was it. Everything died that day. For these past four years, he'd gone through the motions, and counted down the hours till this moment. Of course he had to be strong for the men, he owed them that, and for Veronica, he owed Jim that at least. And now it was almost over. The great Dinny O Brien was moving on. He knew only this. As and from tomorrow night, he would never don the uniform again, but he would always be a warder, for it was in his soul and his bones and his blood... and he was proud of it. With that in mind, he packed away the last of his things and prepared himself for pasture.

Matters in the jail had begun to spiral. There was an air of expectation that harped back to darker times, and the word coming down was not good, not good at all. Information received was that the place was going to blow and that scalps would be had. In the prelude to battle, leaders had emerged and the lines were drawn. At 5.30pm unlock, prisoners bustled into the yards and recreation halls. Inmate 17302, Barry O Shea, made his way from cluster to cluster, plotting, planning, rallying the troops. The staff knew this, of course. This kind of despot was not very discreet, just very dangerous, but to attempt removing him could have sparked the whole thing off. The very least they could expect, was to be kicked stupid by a wing full of adrenalin rushed psychopaths. They'd never make it to safety, so they pulled back and watched from a safe distance.

O Shea was an upstart, a wannabe, but he was in good company. The place was full of them and they burned to go down in the annals of Meadowvale history as a bad crew, mean, cold hearted motherfuckers who would destroy with all the wrath of an Armageddon. It was understood by them all, that Talbot was here for one reason only. He had vowed in the witness stand to finish what he'd started and, courtesy of the Department, here he was to deliver. O Shea had learned that 'The Beast' would be on the move come Monday. That gave him about thirty hours or so, and O Shea was in no doubt that Talbot would be aware of this. Regardless of how many times they were told, some officers still held open conversations by cell doors. It was known by the jailers as The Gulag Telegraph and, of course, there would be those who couldn't resist taunting

Sean Talbot with the news of his imminent departure. O Shea eyeballed them from a distance.

"Smug bastards" he thought "Laugh now you pig fucks, for tomorrow... you... will... die"

Talbot would make his move, and when he did, the blue wing mob would make history. He drew the needle from his arm, and as the crazy lady coursed through his veins, he pictured carnage and bloodshed... and death.

Augustine Mulcahy had some tough decisions to make. The file before him was repulsive. The cynical observations of the governors had put Derek Grady on the edge. A burnt out, wet brained, unstable wreck. Unruly. Insubordinate. *"A man who does not respond appropriately to discipline or supervision"*. A bum. His attendance was sporadic and his punctuality, appalling. Even the reports from the prison psychiatrist were unfavourable. It was stated that *"The erratic behaviour of Derek Grady is symptomatic of post traumatic stress. His experiences during the riots of 1993, and in particular, the guilt he assumes in relation to the death of Prison Officer Francis Hogan will, no doubt, influence his personality throughout his life"* and concludes that *"The subject is an alcoholic and his illness would be better treated in an environment other than that of the prison"*. The report stopped short of recommending his dismissal.

Yet, in 1990, Doc was commended by the Minister for his bravery and initiative in foiling an escape attempt. In 1992, he was offered a promotion, which he refused, and later that year, he sat at the security committee, set up to combat the growing drugs problem at Meadowvale Prison. But, now his future lay in the hands of Chief Officer Mulcahy, and, had he known it, he would not have counted on another year in the service. Augustine had been obsessed with Gradys downfall. He had seen it as a means of stamping his authority on the men, of fulfilling his obligations to the Department, of satisfying his own need for self respect. But things had changed. Ever since his gut wrenching revelation to Eileen and Conor, Augustine had taken a long, hard look in the mirror. Perhaps his obsession had always been there, and Doc had just been dragged to provide some kind of focus for it. And there was the money. Sweet lovin' Jesus, he had stolen that money with the intention of seeing another man swing… and he demanded *respect*!

He thought of the beating Conor had taken, and what may have happened if Doc hadn't come along. He recalled the genuine concern that Derek had shown at the dinner dance when he asked after the boy. He imagined the hurt that Grady must be carrying, and he remembered the torture on his face and the trembling coffee in his hand.

"Doc's trying to get better" he told himself "He's making a fucking effort".

Derek was a sad and lonely soul, just like Augustine had been for all these years. He was trying to unravel the colossal fucking mess, when there was a knock at the door, and Matty Morris stepped in. His expression said it all. They were in big trouble.

"Chief" he said "can I have a word"

His voice was solemn and it frightened Augustine more than a little.

"Yes. Yes Matty, of course. Take a seat"

Matty Morris held a deep breath to calm the jitters. "Chief… we've done a check, and as we stand, we are missing snooker balls, workshop screwdrivers, scissors and knives from the kitchens. Now, that doesn't include whatever syringes and weapons they have stored already. In a nutshell… they are armed to the hilt in there. You've been around a long time, Augustine, and you know what's going to happen here tomorrow. I'm asking you on behalf of the staff, and I'm pleading with you for all that's right, do not unlock this jail in the morning. Wait until Talbot is gone, and we'll deal with the fallout then".

Matty rested his head on the palms of his hands. This was serious shit. Deadly serious.

The wardens would box each other occasionally. A jailer might be changing his long johns in the locker room, when a colleague would dart out from the shadows and crack him across the skull. Scores were settled that way and, generally speaking, they got on with it afterwards. But that tradition was not afforded to Gerard Magner. He had cut many a bad track with the men in his day, and he found himself, this week, laying low for fear that the officers would measure his anus for an electrical fitting. His rush to judgement concerning Gradys guilt had incensed them and hell hath no fury like a warden scorned, so he had taken annual leave on the hope that Docs guilt would be proven and his presumptions would be seen as justified. He had surfaced for air only when he had to, once on his ill-fated meeting with Orr, and on another occasion when he had encountered Pablo Rogers at the grocery store. Rogers had informed him that some yank had shown an interest in Rio Grande and, regardless of the danger to himself, Magner could not pass up the opportunity to offload the site, which he had regarded as a lost cause. Rio Grande was a barren, worthless plot of land that he had accepted from Boss Keane, in part payment of an outstanding loan. Prior to his demise, Boss had been refused credit to expand his 'business interests'. The problem was, he didn't actually have any interests other than the pub, and every bank manager in the area knew it. Magner took the chance, though. Boss had a small farm that he had run into the ground, but Ger saw potential in it. Rio Grande was only ever meant to cover the interest on the loan, but, when Keane dropped dead in the lingerie department of McQuillans shop, the financial institutions carved up what was left of the keane estate, 30 acres of unworkable land, 14 emaciated cows, a badly rusted

Massey Ferguson and a pornography collection, worth more than the rest put together. Magner was left with the site and, if the yank was interested, he could take it off his hands, at a reasonable price, of course. He knocked on the guesthouse door and Mick Roche saw him into the living room.

Mulcahy picked up the phone and dialled the governor. Delahunty answered.

"Governor" said Augustine "it's Mulcahy"

"Ah, Augustine, how are you?" The voice sounded as patronising as usual. "How did last night go. I didn't make it, myself. I was on the television, did you see me?"

"No Governor, I didn't. Look... we have a major situation on our hands, down here. Prisoners are tooled up for one hell of a fight, and this place is going sky high if we unlock in the morning. I think we should hold off till Monday, till Talbot is gone, and, if there's still tension, we can wing it with staff drafted in from other jails"

There was silence on the line. Augustine wasn't sure Delahunty hadn't hung up on him.

"Governor... are you there""Oh, I'm here alright, Mulcahy" barked Murtagh "but I can't believe the shit that I'm hearing. Wing it, did you say? Fucking wing it. Listen... BOY, I have responsibilities, and prisoners have rights. Are you with me so far? These men look on us as their guardians, as their... caretakers, if you will. We operate under the very eye of public scrutiny, and people rely on me to ensure that we maintain a civil, humane environment for the poor misfortunes in our care. And you want me to tell Joe fucking Ordinary that, when the chips are down, we… wing it. Get a hold of yourself, man. You will unlock the prison tomorrow and Monday and Tuesday, and every other fucking day thereafter. Do I make myself clear, Mulcahy?"

He sounded like some demented school principle, and Augustine found his resolve starting to waver under an old, familiar pressure, but he persisted.

"Governor" he said "would you do me the courtesy of coming here tomorrow morning, and addressing the men? I think they deserve that anyway" That was it. Delahunty blew.

"Fuck the men, do you hear me, fuck them. They deserve nothing. A bunch of fucking drunks, shur, didn't you say so yourself? Tomorrow, I'll be live on Vale FM, and if there's one word of trouble, just one, I'll come down there and drive a steel toe cap up your hole, Mulcahy. Now, FUCK OFF like a good little man!" and he slammed the phone down.

Augustine went to explain, but Matty indicated that he had heard the lot. The Chief stared at his shoes for a second, unable to make eye contact. He had, indeed, referred to the men as drunks, and he found himself embarrassed now, regretful. He understood them better since he had stopped… pretending.

"Right" he said "where do we go from here?" and they sat in silence, staring at each other.

Bradford Shaw was stunned. He had expected that Magner might be hard nosed, but this was ridiculous.

"£20,000, you can't be serious"

"You know" said Ger "you sounded just like John McEnroe, there. And, yes, I'm serious. That's prime land we're talking about. If you only knew the amount of investors interested in Rio Grande, you'd be shocked"

"So, why is it still for sale, then, if all these investors are kicking in your door?"

"Well, I have a sense of community, you see, that would not allow me sell that site if it were not in the best interests of the town. Men came up here not two weeks ago, throwing twice that much at me, but I had to decline. They wanted to open a lap dancing club, and I just wouldn't have it. You seem like such a sincere man... let me see... let's call it... £17,000 and we have ourselves a deal"

It may as well have been £170,000, Bradford didn't have it. The Army had not allowed for dreams when they paid him off, and with medical expenses and such like, he was on his uppers. He had the house in the States, but he had hoped that if Magner was reasonable, he might sell that property in order to fund a modest home on the land of his forefathers. Alas, it was not to be, and when Ger

**had gone, he went to his room to prepare for his flight back home on Tuesday.**

(v)   **COMES THE DARK**

The tavern was ablaze with their insanity. They huddled together, like polar cap kings, backs against the storm, feeding off each others unrest. Every so often, someone would run, naked, through the crowd, not caring if they made it to safety. They rarely did. At one point, Sergeant O Driscoll burst through the doors and shouted "This is a bust", before ripping his shirt open to reveal his rose tinted man breasts. Ollie Byrne drew a contorted face on his brothers bare arse, and Pablo stuck a cigar in it, before Mick waddled to the bar, backwards, and let his buttocks order a round. Phelim O Toole climbed onto Tony Ennis' shoulders and declared Viagra a modern miracle, raising a heavily inflamed hand in the air as evidence of his rejuvenated lust for self pleasure. It was crazy.

Dinny and Veronica arrived and they were plied with liquor from all sides. Men stood in queues to shake his hand and kiss her cheek. It was wonderful. They were wonderful. Matty hovered over them and sang 'Martha', while Percy broke out a bottle of champagne and filled their glasses. Such was the affection that they enjoyed. Nora and Victor paid their respects, and Sean rocked in time to the music. Bradford made an appearance, and sparked off a row. Mick Byrne felt that Seans wheelchair was by far the sportier model, while Ollie opted for

Shaws 'American dream'. They took it to the streets. In a scene to rival Ben Hur, they barrelled through the town with their charges, a whoopin' and a hollerin'. The townsfolk came out to cheer them on, and the winning pair of Sean and Ollie enjoyed the applause of the entire pub on their triumphant return.

Doc Grady had imbibed enough black coffee to pole vault for Ireland and, having discussed the Magner/Orr issue with Nora, he headed for home. He climbed the poorly lit stairs to his bedsit and he shuffled inside. Without the juice to ease his solitude, he found the loneliness unbearable. Preferring the darkness, he did not switch on the light. Instead, he sat in the murky shadows of his one roomed existence and called up the faces that had scarred his soul. He could see them clearly. In the bloodshed and the anguish, in the laughter and long goodbyes, they drifted past, like scenes from an old home reel. And there he was. For the first time in some time, Francis Hogans tortured features emerged from the night and accused him of the deed. But Derek Grady could run no more. He was tired and broken up. He reached into the dark and whispered.

"It wasn't me Francy" and he tasted his own sorrow "Things just got so fucked up. But I tried, man, you know that. Now, I've gotta get on with this. You see, I lived, but I forgot about that for such a long time. You go on and rest now, but I'll always remember you like it was in the good days, my friend, and I'll see you soon" Francis Hogan smiled and faded out... forever. Doc tuned his wireless to the blues of the night, and rested.

When the knock came, he was reluctant to respond. He would not be good company, he thought, but he answered it anyway. He opened the door... and he froze. Jean Cooke beamed back at him.

"Hello Derek" she said, and he burst into tears.

He told her of the money and the station, of the jail and Mulcahy, of the demons and the drink. He told her how much he loved her, how badly he had missed her and he told her of how he was fighting back. She had heard it all from Dinny, but she cradled him in the dark and hung on his every word. They shared this night, and, as Dorothy Moore turned their whole world misty blue, they dreamed... together.

Mulcahy stood in the doorway of his sons bedroom, and watched him sleep. He desperately wanted to wake Conor up, to hold him, to kiss his brow, to tell him just how important he was, but he couldn't. He dare not. The new ground was still shaky with him, but he *would* be a better father. Actually, for the first time, he would be a father, he supposed. There were big changes on the way, and he asked God for the strength to see them through. If he could just get tomorrow over with, things could be great. But that was if. He fixed the blankets about his child and went to Eileen.

Denis O Brien and Veronica Gilmore stared at the night sky from the comfort of his double bed. They were at peace. At peace with themselves, at peace with the world, at peace with one another and, as the warm breeze caressed their naked shells, their spirits danced and played and laughed in a kingdom far, far away. Veronica ran her fingers across his flesh, and her nails tickled the contours of his chest and cage. She whispered across his shoulder, and they were like young things.

"Is that for me?" she asked.

He smiled. "Yes ma'am, I do believe it is" and the stillness was interrupted with laughter... laughter and foolishness.

A hush descended on the village, and the heat of the day became the coolness of the witching hour. A calmness enveloped their world, the world of the Meadowvale men, and they welcomed it. They could accept it for what it was, and enjoy it for the brief time it spent with them. They had felt it before. It was the calm that descends when the last minute nerves have gone, the calm of resignation, the calm of knowing, implicitly, that this was indeed the calm before the storm. What they did not know, however, was what, exactly, that storm would hold for each of them.

## CHAPTER FOUR: SUNDAY

(i)     THE FUTURE

The morning brought its own conflict. Before the cock crowed on Meadowvale, the sun battled to find its way through, but dark grey clouds waded in and the fight was short lived. By 7am, great baubles of rain tapped on their windows and demanded their attention. The lazy haze of Saturday was dismissed, but a heavy, sticky heat clung to everything, dripped from everyone and the air was dead and dirty and damp.

Doc Grady opened his eyes and a bead of sweat crept in. It hurt like hell. He shot up, still groggy, and surveyed his surroundings through the untainted optic. He found himself very much alone. It had been a dream, it seemed. Jean had come back to him, to make it all better. She had kissed his face and stroked his hair to make the phantoms disappear, and he had lay in her arms, unafraid. He had imagined it so often that he should have been used to it by now, that moment of bitter loneliness, but reality cut so awfully deep and he was terribly wounded. He was staggering round his shitty little kitchen, when she came up behind him, from the bathroom, and held him like she might never again have the chance to do so. And though the expression on his face suggested differently, the hurting had stopped.

There were no promises, only maybes, but that was a giant step for mankind as far as he was concerned. She pleaded with him to stay, to abandon the jail for her, but he understood the lines that had been drawn in the gaol, and, believing that this day held yet another grim passage in the history of meadowvale, he talked only of tomorrow. Tomorrow and the next day and the next. When he had gone, she wiped the condensation from the window, and watched him fight against the deluge, and there was that old, familiar scene, the thumbs up, the reassuring wave. Perhaps, today would be the first day of the rest of their lives... perhaps, it would be the last.

The toast had gone cold, but he hadn't noticed, and she had been talking for ages, hovering about the sink, but he hadn't heard a word. It was only when she had asked a question, and he had not replied, that she turned to find him, almost hypnotised at the breakfast table. She was worried for him. These past few days, he had become withdrawn, gone into a shell, and she had found it nigh on impossible to reach him.

"Augustine, will you please talk to me" and the tremble in her voice seemed to startle him somewhat.

"Huh… I'm sorry, what was that?" He was only touching down, when he noticed her tears, and he was holding Eileen, consoling her, when Conor walked in.

"It's okay, son" he said, sensing the boys hesitation, and he beckoned him to his side. Augustine Mulcahy, who knew not how to love, who hid for a lifetime behind the ugly scars of hatred, embraced his family in the early hours of a stormy Sunday.

Dinny struggled to keep his trousers up, while Veronica Gilmore endeavoured to keep them down. They went at it, to and fro, for a while till she gave in. At breakfast, they talked of the future and what it held for them. Today was the big one. The *last* shift. The great Denis O Brien, jailer extraordinaire, would be but a memory. He was terrified. What would become of him. Out side the walls of the jail, he'd be an old age pensioner… a fucking bus pass holder. He could see himself, fumbling with the crumbs of hot crossed buns and penning his way through bingo cards, while some young filly in a nurses uniform, dabbed the tea stains from his chin. Veronica thought this was hilarious. While he had been ambling down memory lane, and preparing himself for the old folks home, she had been busy.

With Jim Gilmores life insurance policy, God rest him, and Dinnys golden handshake, they were actually worth a pretty penny. She sat him down and demanded his attention. She did not see them finish their days by the sea, or in the sun. There would be no afternoon tea parties, or golden day outings. She had bigger plans. Percival Richards, she felt, had suffered enough. The poor man had worn a torment on his face that was hard to look at sometimes, and it was only decent and proper that someone take away his anguish. In the morning they would begin negotiations for the tavern. 'The Jailers Rest', as it would be called, would provide them with the opportunity to carry on as they always had, catering for the needs of the Meadowvale warders, the men and women who were sown into the fabric of their lives. Dinny would not, so much, be leaving, he would be, merely, crossing the counter. Yes indeed, she had great plans. 'The Jailers Rest', proprietors Denis and Veronica O Brien.

"Does this mean… " he began, but she cut him off.

"Now, you don't think that I'm going to live in sin, at my age, mister"

He thought of wild nights and crazy days, of reunions and old tales, and of their future, their wonderful, incredible future. He held her softly and kissed her. "I do" he said, and he got up to face the world. Before he left, she launched one last assault on his belt buckle. This time she won.

(ii)    **THE LONGEST TIME**

Sister Gertrude had been a personal friend to the prisoners of Meadowvale for over five years. Two or three times a week, she would come to the jail and offer them her guidance. They would sit with her, and talk endlessly about their screwed up parents or their banged up wives or their fucked up kids or, indeed, of the heartless men and women who deprived them of their liberty at the end of each day. They were sorry for the rapes and the murders, for the muggings and the beatings, for the drug deals and depravities, but no good in worrying about that now, you can't change the past. That most of them insisted on destroying someones life as soon as they were released, really was of no concern to the good Sister. God had made her gullible, and she liked it that way. Another soul for Jesus, hallelujah and praise the Lord.

She would sneak in parcels and packages that they were not allowed, and she would carry out with her, coded messages that she never understood, to the screwed up parents and to the banged up wives and to the fucked up kids. It made her feel important, like she belonged, like she was needed. It was her calling. She had not been in Meadowvale when Sean Talbot did what he did. She did not know the men who died or their parents or their wives or their kids. They were not important to her because she was not important to them, and if there was a spiritual term for 'fuck them' she would have used it. After all, men who get locked up get tense. Of course they do, and sometimes that tension spills over. It's to be expected. Prison Officers know that, so why the song and dance when things go wrong. At the end of the day, misguided creatures end up in prison because society did not understand them like she did, but jailers are there of their own free will. Now, what kind of person dose that?

Sean Talbot and those other boys must have been driven onto the roof, forced into making a stand, and when the officers went up there, all gung ho, the prisoners got frightened and bad things happened. It was true, the officers didn't deserve to die, but, shur, God has them and that makes it all okay. She had received a message from a trustee inmate in the segregation unit, that Talbot had expressed an interest in visiting the chapel today, and that he had specifically asked for her counsel. She was coming to Meadowvale to save the immortal soul of Sean Talbot, the beast. What a disgusting thing to call another human being, a child of Jaweh. He must feel so humiliated, that the world had been so unjust with him. She arrived in the jail at 8am to deliver him into the loving arms of Christ. The boss would be so happy.

On morning parade, the staff lined up outside the prison, and Mulcahy called their names from a list. As each officers name was broadcast, they replied "Anseo" and they were marked in, present and correct. When they were finished, Augustine addressed them. Sensing their anger, he told them that the order to unlock had come from a higher authority. He told them to be careful, to watch out for one and other, and not to take chances. If anything were to happen, they were to get out and not leave anyone behind. He said that all that was expected of them, was that they do their duty and he wished them all luck. He wanted to let them know that he was afraid too, that he had a family waiting for him just as they had and that he had been awake all night worrying, but he said none of those things. They did not like him. They thought that he was a prick, and he hadn't given them any reason to doubt it. He fixed his peak and went to the chiefs office. He had assumed that the rank brought its own respect, but, now, he understood that he would have to earn it. Nobody deserves respect automatically, not even educated men. The chief was growing up.

Matty Morris was standing at the entrance to the green wing, when Tony Ennis descended on him, asking what in the fuck was going on. Matty said that he did not know what in the fuck was going on, so Tony filled him in. Sister Gertrude had told the staff in the segregation unit, that Sean Talbot was to be brought to the chapel when the other prisoners were finished with Sunday mass. She said that Governor Delahunty had agreed it and, that anyway, the laws of God overruled the will of man. She said that she would speak with Talbot alone, and that the staff were to stay far enough away, so as to allow the beast a private word with his maker.

Doc Grady had been A.W.O.L for a day or two, and he found himself sifting through the officers mail at the jail sorting office, in the hope, perhaps, that somebody somewhere would be interested in his well being. With the exception of Dinny, no one had *really* watched out for him after Jean left and, considering his sordid descent on the juice, Denis had carried him about like a bird with a broken wing. With everything that was going on, he hadn't found the time to thank the big guy, but he would. He thumbed his way through the post, but, although there was nothing of interest to him, he did locate a suprising amount of correspondence for Ger Magner. There were six envelopes addressed to him, each

one carrying the logo of the local tourist board. The issue of the Hegartys had played onDocs mind, since he had spoken to Nora. What business did Magner have with this fucker, David Orr, and why would anybody from the town have reason to complain Sean to the authorities? Everyone knew the story there, and people felt genuine concern for him. That slimy prick, Magner, was up to his bollox in something nasty, and Doc aimed to find out what. He bundled Magners post together, and stuffed it in his pocket.

Bradford Shaw was really going to miss Meadowvale. The place was insane, and he loved it. Great chunks of last night were a blur to him, and he had woken up this morning to find a strange lady in the bed, beside him. At breakfast, she introduced herself as Bridget, and said that she worked in the jail. Apparently, she had found him charming, charming enough to wheel him home and physically carry him over her shoulder to the boudoir. She informed him, with only a hint of a blush, that they had "had a right good goot" and, that regardless of whether he was crippled or not, he showed no signs of, what she poetically described as "fever sag". A few short days ago, he was perched by a window in Lincoln, Nebraska, waiting for death to do him a favour, now, here he was, an historical sleuth, in the motherland, drinking, gooting and defying fever sag. On Wednesday, when he would board the flight to America, he would not be going home, he felt, he would be leaving it.

Mulcahy was just about to sit at his desk, when Matty burst into his office, yelling at him about riots and deaths and history repeating itself. He took Augustine quite by surprise, and the chief staggered backward, almost falling over his chair on the way. He shouted at Matty to calm down, but to no avail. Morris was electric, and there was a moment of pandemonium as the two men attempted to scream each other down. Eventually, Augustine learned of Sister Gertrudes instruction to the segregation unit staff.

"Now Chief" said Matty, "if we bring that murdering bastard through an unlocked jail… "

But he never got the chance to finish. Mulcahy was charging down the hall in search of the nun.

Phelim O Toole approached the Movieland Twins, as they watched the inmates emerge from their cells. They were standing at the circle end of YW2, which was the second floor of the yellow wing, adjacent to the chapel entrance. Church was not high on the agenda of the prison population, and only a handful of convicts, travellers mostly, made their way to God, this Sunday morning. The Byrne brothers were deep in conversation when Phelim arrived, and they got straight to business. They were angry at Delahunty for ordering an unlock under such tense conditions, and they thought that O Toole might have an insight into his motives.

"You are a union man" said Ollie "What the fuck is he playing at?"

"Have you seen his car?" asked Phelim

Ollie thought for a second.

"A strange question, but, yes. I have seen his car and it's a piece of shit"

"Well" said Phelim "have you never wondered why a senior Governor, on that kind of salary, drives a fuckin' rustbucket like that?"

Of course they had all heard the stories. Delahunty was a notorious gambler, an out and out addict. His losses at the track were legendary, but that still didn't explain why he had put the lives of every officer in jeopardy.

"I'll put it to you this way" said Phelim, and he cleared his throat "A friend of mine saw himat the races in Tralee, one day, and he told me that Delahunty lost five or six grand in little over an hour. Five or six fucking grand, boys, and that was just in Tralee. Now, I don't care what kind of sheckles you're on, nobody can afford a hit like that. So, work it out for yourselves. When someone goes in over their head for huge dollars, like he must be, whose pockets do you think they would find themselves in?"

"The dirtbirds" said Mick.

"The dirtbirds exactly" exclaimed Phelim "And not the no marks like these fellas" and he pointed at the cells "No, you are in it up to your fuckin' gonads with the big guys. You owe a debt to the crime bosses, and who works for the crime bosses?"

"The dirtbirds" said Mick.

"The dirtbirds exactly" said Phelim "The 2 by 4 fucking scangers that we have here in Meadowvale. So, good ole Murtagh is under instruction to take care of the lads, and no one will come looking for his kneecaps. He can run up a tab in every racecourse in the country, and, so long as these motherfuckers get taken care of, no one gives a shit" He took a long drag of his cigarette and pulled it in.

"So, there you have it, boys and girls, we are all part of the same gang"

Ollie thought about it and shook his head.

"But, if that's all true, then why do the department allow him to run a major institution like this?"

"Because" said Phelim "he's the public face of the prison service. Have you ever watched him bullshit on television. All he is short of doing is healing the lepers and raising the dead. All that crap about sitting in cells, holding their fucking hands, shur, that prick wouldn't know how to open a cell door. When was the last time anybody actually saw him in the jail. There are half decent chaps in here waiting months to see him, and they'll have beards down to their nuts by the time that they do. He is up there in his ivory tower, trouserless, talking to Joe Dolan, like some fucking loon. He's a mad, bad bastard for sure, but the public think that he is the second coming, and the department couldn't buy that kind of P.R."

The brothers were fired up. Phelim had a way of doing that to the men, and they loved it. Nothing like a good blood boiler to get things going.

"By Jaysus, but you're on the ball, O Toole" said Ollie "That filthy bastard, and he on the papers or the radio saying that these fellas are societies problem and not just his. Is each member of society on his salary, to deal with a problem that he is employed to sort out? No they fucking well are not, and you know what the gas part of it is, they agree with him. Isn't that something?"

"And that, my friends" said Phelim "is why he is kept in charge of Meadowvale. Now, give me one of them fags, before I burst"

Eileen Mulcahy stood by her son, and they stared in the mirror. She fixed his bow tie and straightened his blazer. He looked super and she told him so.

"Your father is going to be so proud of you, Conor, but remember, you'll only be with him for an hour, so don't get under his feet. He is a very important man in there, and not every little boy gets to see the inside of a prison"

Conor did not care about every other little boy. Today was the best day ever. His dad had called him "son" and he had hugged him, and now he was going to spend time with him at work. He might even meet that nice Mr. Grady again. "Things are going to get better, love" she said, and she kissed his rosy cheeks. "Your father is going to see to that"

They both felt the excitement, and it showed.

It came as no shock to Sister Gertrude when the Chief Officer stormed in and started laying down the law. He was a notorious pig, by all accounts, and she understood that he would be unhappy about the lack of consultation on such an issue. It was the usual bullshit about staff safety and security, so while he was in full flow, she dialled the Governor and handed Mulcahy her phone.

Delahuntys patience with Augustine was growing thin and he was angry. Angry that his authority had come into question yet again, angry that the Chief had sided with the Officers and angry that he had been contacted as he sat in the hallway of Vale FM, where he was desperately displaying his happy head for the public. It would not look good for the Florence Nightingale of the nick if he were to scream at his men, to call them all useless piles of shit, to threaten them with transfers or worse, so between the smiles and the high hand salutes, he *whispered* obscenities and ultimatums to Mulcahy.

When he handed the mobile to Sister Gertrude, Augustine was humiliated and degraded. He shuffled from side to side, not knowing what to say, and sensing his pain, Tony Ennis called on the Chief to tend to an issue in the unit office. Away from the nauseam of the nuns smugness, he sat him down and handed him a coffee.

"I would give you something stronger" said Tony "only I know that you wouldn't take it. We appreciate what you tried to do, Chief, but I could have told you that was going to happen. The Officer gets fucked for fun, and so it has always been, but thanks anyway"

The good Sister decided to check in on Talbot, to make sure that the filthy screws weren't mistreating him. They knew nothing of forgiveness, she imagined, and they had probably tormented him since he came. She lifted the flap that covered the cell door observation point, and she stared inside. It was dark. Too dark to see anything clearly. A jail towel was draped across the cell window, and it blocked most daylight from entering. Perhaps Talbot did not like the sun, not that there was any. It was grey enough to be evening, and the rain pelted down, drowning out the normal commotion of the prison. She couldn't see him, and she wanted to reassure him, so she tapped on the glass and called out. A sliver of light fell across his bed, and she could just about make out an arm, a tee shirt perhaps, she was not sure. She called out again.

"Sean, can you here me? It's Sister Gertrude"

There was movement and she caught something reflected on the beams of light that had, somehow, side stepped the towel. She squinted to get a better look and then... she froze. He was staring at her. His shaven head was unnatural, grotesque, in the dim, and the eyes, the *black* eyes, the *dead* eyes captured her in their gaze and growled with a menace that she had only read of in the testaments, and, at that moment, she understood his name. She backed away. Her voice barely broke a whisper and a tremble swayed on it.

"I'll need Officers" she said "Lots of them. I don't care if you can spare them or not. They will be in the chapel, at the altar, beside me. Make it so" and she went to the church to ask God for strength.

Talbot faded back into the dark. A radio cassette player lay on the bed beside him, and he stroked its contours lovingly, as if there was a moment to be shared. He tapped, lightly, on each corner and the casing gave way. Guarding his movements fromprying eyes, he delicately stripped the box of its trappings and allowed his fingers to slip inside. They ran along the diodes and the circuits to the battery compartment, where they sliced upon the razors edge of the knife concealed therein. He felt the warm trickle of his own blood against the cold steel, and he grinned. It was showtime.

Brad Shaw imagined that he had broken a rib. He had vague recollections of Bridget lifting him, naked, from the bed and body slamming him against the wall. She was a powerful woman, was Bridget, and he had to say that, all in all, the experience had not been without its moments. When she left that morning, she had patted his buttocks and tucked the blankets in around him.

"Sleep General" she had said to him "You're gonna need your strength"

He liked her. She was a strong willed, highly charged, wrecking ball of a gal and a man of his fibre responded well to her discipline. He thought that he might make his way out to Rio Grande, if the weather softened, but there was no sign of that, so he dressed, ate breakfast and wandered out to catch Sunday service at the Drumasheen chapel. No harm in staying on the right side of the big fella. After all, there was a part of him, a very small part albeit, that harboured thoughts of divine intervention. The prayer meeting had, on occasion, thrown up a contentious miracle or two, and Monday nights group would be his last chance to tap dance. He wasn't holding his breath. In the aftermath of the Persian Gulf conflict, he had rubbed wheels with far too many ex servicemen, all trying to find Jesus in nursing home corridors of that forgotten America. They had parted company with their eyes or their legs or their souls in the napalm and the scuds and the midnight mortars of democracies great campaigns. In his heart, he had run away from it. He was still running.Doc was trying to piece it all together. The letters from the tourist board had discussed Ger Magners plans for the property at 37 Quinlans hill, Meadowvale. Magner was hoping to have it registered on their official guesthouse list, and there was talk of the property being graded early in the new year. Doc was not aware that number 37 was for sale and, to the best of his knowledge, Nora Hegarty had plans of her own for the place, so what the fuck was Magner at. There was no way that she would take Sean out of the area. He would not have the ability, now, to adapt to somewhere new, and he was much loved and cared for by those in the town who had known him before the accident. Then, of course, there was the issue of David Orr. If he was to have his way, Sean would be gone by the end of the week anyway, so those concerns would become irrelevant. Doc felt terribly sorry for Nora. Without her boy, she would fall to pieces, no doubt about it. She had the respect of the whole town for the way she cared for him. A lesser creature might have folded long before now, but she was a tough lady and little shits like Orr and Magner would have to come up with something special to take her down. He lit a cigarette and thought hard. Orr and Magner... Orr... and... Magner, and in the swirling grey curls of a burning John Player, it became a little clearer. Orr and fucking Magner, the horrible bastards, they were in it together. Of course they were, shur, didn't he catch them together. Oh my God, was Ger Magner really that evil. Here they were, worrying about the dirtbirds, when the biggest fucking scumbag of them all was wearing a uniform, AND HE WAS PROMOTED. Good fuck. He would have to speak with Nora and Victor Roberts. He would catch them at lunchtime, and they would sort this out. He was about to leave the tea room, when Dinny walked in.Mass was ended and the travelling community of Meadowvale Prison went in peace to love and serve the Lord. The entire jail was unlocked, and Officers stood as close to the wing exits as possible. They knew that with the torrential rain, it was unlikely that the prisoners would go to the exercise yards, so the hope was that the recreation halls would be used. At least if something were to go wrong, the inmates would be contained. The heat was becoming unbearable and the jailers baked in the oven. Their shirts were sweat soaked, and they pulled at their collars, hoping for a respite that did not come. There was an edge and it was obvious. They stayed in clusters, never straying, and there was little conversation for fear that they would miss some vital element that might later be seen as the moment it blew. Weapons could move through fifty or sixty pairs of hands, and could be carried right past you without your knowledge. The first time that you were made aware of a blade was, very often, when it was slicing your face open, and the melted sugar from a flask of boiling water could be peeling the flesh off your skull while you are still checking the time. Such is the way of the Gaol. It was all nice and dandy for Mulcahy to say that they should get out if the place erupted, but that meant running the gauntlet, and a warder could be carved up like a pig before the gate was in sight. There were too many Officers with the scars to prove it.

Female Officers were not allowed on the wings, that day. Everyone knew what the prisoners would do if they could take a sheezer hostage. An convict who had not seen a real ladies curves in some years, could become a might insensitive when he got to fumbling with a uniform skirt, or indeed a jail trousers. Many of these men had enjoyed each others rectums on long winters nights, and a male officers arse would be like a moose head over the fireplace, a scalp, a trophy, something to tell the boys about when they pass around their HIV needles and share the hit. Get them into the Rec. halls and let this horrible fucking day be over. They had never looked forward to Percys therapy quite so badly.

Doc was surprised to see Dinny. With everything that was happening in the jail, it was expected that he would be a no-show for today. It was not as if the management could write to him for the absence.

"I have to admire your commitment" said Derek "but you're a foolish man to be spending your last hours as a warder in a shithole like this"

"Well, where else would a jailer be if not in a jail, shithole or not? I have done this for longer than I care to remember, Doc, and come eight o clock this evening, I'll walk out those gates a free man. I'm going to enjoy it, son"

Doc took the opportunity to pay his respects. He wanted to hold the hand that had carried him for so long, and he knew that Dinny had made the call that had brought Jean back to him. He stood up and embraced the great man whole heartedly, if not a little awkwardly. They were no good at that kind of thing. Usually, they would indicate their admiration in bear hugs and free beer, the other thing was for the women, but Doc felt the gesture was appropriate in a father and son kind of way.

"Thanks for everything, Din, you're one of the good guys. I am so sorry for all the shite that I put you through"

It was true. Like the song says, you always hurt the ones you love, and Doc must have loved Denis in heaps. There were nights when he was so far out of his head that his intoxication and his aggression would have an empty corner in the busy tavern, just for him. But Dinny would take the abuse and the slaps and see him home, peel the shitty kecks off him and tidy the whore up, wash the blood from his face when it was needed and leave water and painkillers beside his bed for the hangover. But he did not do so for the applause.

"Stop that, for fuck sake, lad. You would have done the same for me"

But Doc needed to get it out.

"No, Dinny, no. I have been an albatross round everyones neck for these past few years, especially yours, and I am going to be apologising for the rest of my service but, fuck it, credit where it's due. Denis O Brien, *you* are the man and that *is* a fact"

Dinny was waving his arms for Doc to stop. They owed each other nothing. The day that they started banking credits on each other would be a sad day indeed. They would just get on with it, together and Doc agreed.

"She came back last night" said Doc "But I'm sure you knew that"

Dinny smiled. "I thought she might", and Doc told him the story.

It was great. He stood up and walked around and sat down and stood up again, as he recounted his tale and Dinny thought that he had not seen Derek this alive, this human, since long before Jean had left.

"Welcome home, friend" he said "It's good to have you back"

"And you" laughed Doc "Look at you, steppin' out with the girls. I'll bet Mammy O Brien, God rest her, would have got some shock if she walked into your place and tripped over a pair of Veronicas drawers" and he suddenly realised what he had said.

"Christ Dinny, I didn't mean to say that"

"Will you fucking give over" said Denis "Shur, if my mother had ever found a pair of Veronicas kecks, she would have jumped straight into them and gone lookin' for my father. I found a pair of the auld ones knickers one day and, honest to Jesus, they looked like they had been tarmacadamed"

They talked of the past, and reflected on the future. The events of the day played no part in it. Doc told him that Veronica had been a friend to them all, at one time or another, and that the men and women of Meadowvale owed them both a great debt of gratitude.

"She has, indeed" said Dinny "She has been good for me too, which is the reason that we have agreed to jump the broom. Now, you are the first to know, so don't go shouting your mouth off about it, alright?"

But Doc was upon him, swinging out off his hand and slapping his back.

"Ah Jaysus, that's super. I am over the moon for the pair of youse" and his elation was electric "Well fuck me anyway, but that's dynamite. Good on ya big guy"

"Well" said Dinny "I guess that I've been married to the wrong things all my life. When I was a kid, I was married to the farm, broke my bollox till the father lost it to the bank. When Jim ended up with Veronica, I married the job and now, finally, I have gotten this one chance and, I can tell you, that I am going to make up for lost time" and he told Doc of their plans for the bar.

The phone call came through from Sister Gertrude, to say that Talbot should now be brought to the chapel. The question was how. How were they to get this over with, without having to march 'The Beast' through a pressure cooker prison. There was a way, perhaps. Yes... it could work. It *must* work. Just outside the unit, there was an entrance to the tradesmens tunnel. The tunnel ran under the jail, and housed the telephone system, a generator room and one or two old store rooms, but it ran to the front steps of the jail. They could, in theory anyway, take him through there and, when they came out at the far end, they could escort him to the chapel using an emergency entrance to the rear of the church. When it was all over with, they could bring him back the same way, avoiding any contact with the animals upstairs. Anyway, it was the only chance that they had to avert an almost certain riot, and if Talbot wanted to meet Jesus, he would have to get down to get up.

Mulcahy ordered Tony Ennis to get the tunnel entrance keys and told the segregation unit staff to get ready for the move. Officer Peter Woods went on ahead and opened the back stairs gate to the chapel. Several staff were detailed to be present at the altar, for when they arrived, and Augustine thought to himself that if they could just get the operation over with, everything would be fine. The whole thing should not take more than forty five minutes, an hour at worst. Between them all, they should be able to contain him, even if the Sister had specified that no handcuffs. The man was not to meet his maker in restraints, and Delahunty had agreed. That said, he would be held securely, and once they had him back in his cell, he would stay there till morning and he'd be gone. When Tony arrived back with the keys, Mulcahy checked with each man to make sure that he was happy with the arrangements.

"I realise" he said "that this whole fucking mess stinks, and I *will* understand it if any of you want to pull out now. This is a terrible situation that you are asked to find yourselves in, and I wont hold it against any of you, should you walk away now" He pointed at the forboding sight of the tunnel. "We are going to have to go through hell to get to heaven, men, and I would, personally, prefer to be at home with my wife and child right now, so, just say the word and I'll have you replaced with someone else" But no one did, and they removed the beast from his cell, and descended into the dark.

Eileen and Conor Mulcahy arrived at the gate of Meadowvale Jail, for their family visit. Eileen was well known to the staff, and they were directed to the Chiefs office, but to Conor, this was all very new. Apart from his father, he had never actually seen another Prison Officer in uniform, and he was convinced that he saw Augustine every time a warder shot past. As they approached the front steps of the prison, Eileen remembered that they had not signed the visitors book at the main gate. She would not like to see the staff in any kind of trouble with administration, so she told Conor to stay put nearby and she darted off to register them.

In the few moments while she was gone, Conor got nervous. He felt uncomfortable on his own. A place like Meadowvale could be daunting enough for an adult, but for a child it was downright terrifying. There were bad people here, bad like in the movies. They would say things like "you dirty rat" and "put up yer dukes, wise guy, I'm runnin' this show, see", and sometimes a fella could get slugged in the kisser for whistling at the photograph of another guys dame. Conor had no interest in running the show or stealing dames, but they might not know that. He was starting to panic, when he saw his father disappear through an open door to the side of the front steps. He was sure it was him, he was wearing the hat and everything. He called out, but Augustine did not reply. Perhaps he had not heard him. Conor made his way to the opening, and stared inside. It was dark and he could not see very far. He wanted to follow his father, but he was terrified of the dark. It reminded him of the space under his bed at night, always too afraid to look, always too always too petrified not to.

He was about to go in search of Eileen, when he heard voices in the shadows. They were unclear and they seemed to echo like they were coming from a cave or a deep pit, but one of the voices sounded just like his father. Yes, he was sure now, he could definitely hear Augustine in the dim. A huge surge of relief swept over Conor, and he stepped inside the open doorway and crept into the gloom.

Mulcahy was sweating heavily and his heart pounded against the walls of his chest. He was convinced that the other men could hear it, but, if they did, they did not let on. They were too busy listening to the hammers in their own hearts, and trying to stay on their feet, as they shuffled along the path in the deathly night of the tunnel. When they saw it up ahead, they were not concerned. It appeared to be the entrance to one of the store rooms, and whoever had been down here earlier, had forgotten to lock it up. The door lay open and they were only too happy to avail of the bulb lighting, poor though it was. It caused only a minor problem. Were they to pass it unlocked, it would mean having to change their formation and, for containment purposes, it was imperative that they keep an even body of men around Talbot. Augustine ordered them to stop, while Tony Ennis went on ahead to lock it up.

It should not have been a problem. It should not have caused them any difficulty what so ever. It should not have been something that stayed with them for the rest of their lives… but it would be. Before Tony never got the chance to close the stupid fucking door, he was stopped dead in his tracks by the trembling, petrified voice of a child calling out in the dark for his father. It was chilling. It should not be there, could not be there, had no place being there, but it was there. Clear as day, it was there, frightened, alone, lost. They half expected to see the phantom of some poor soul, float from the shadows, twisted and bloodied, but instead they were presented with the incredible sight of a small, round boy in a blazer and a bow tie, whose eyes were swollen and glazed with fear.

Waves of shock cut through the Chief and his heart tipped over and plummeted to the pits of his stomach. Eileens voice called out from the farthest reaches of his mind.

"He misses you when you're not here" she was saying "Why don't you bring him with you on Sunday, just for an hour. Spend some time together. You need that too"

For a moment they were all distracted, and just for that moment, they forgot why they were there. But Talbot didn't, and if ever there was an opportunity for payback, this was it. As Augustine reached out for his son and broke the circle, Sean 'The Beast' Talbot, killer of screws and defiler of women, removed the knife from his underpants and charged past. The child was his now, and for the first time, he felt the beating of his own heart, but unlike the others, he throbbed with the excitement and the ecstasy that was the rapturous surge of revenge. He grabbed the boy around his throat and pulled Conors head back against his own chest. The young Mulcahy felt the cold razor against his windpipe, and there was an unbearable pain as the first snake of blood slithered along the blade and seeped into the collar of his freshly pressed shirt. He screamed out in agony, but to no avail. He was dragged inside the store room and he felt his new trousers snag and rip forever on a sharp edge that he did not see. The last thing that he did see, however, before the door was pulled in on top of him, was his father, kicking and screaming at a group of uniformed men who were trying to restrain him... and the long night followed.

(iii)   JESUS, IT'S HOT

Prisoner Barry O Shea paced back and forth on the landing. He was agitated. This shit had better kick off soon, or had 'The Beast' gone soft and found God or Buddha or some such can of piss. He had gone out on a limb here, promised the lads some real fireworks. They were ready, ready as they were ever going to be, and if this did not happen today, they were likely to throw their hats at it. Right now, he had the chance to be the man, tomorrow he would just be another fucking no mark with an attitude. All they needed was the news that 'The Beast' had lived up to his reputation, and as soon as that came down, they would rip this stinking shithole to pieces. Meadowvale would burn, along with all of the motherfuckers that ran it, you just wait and see. He stopped pacing and went to join the others.

Harry Ryan had been a reporter for The Chronicle since the eighties. He was loosely referred to as the crime correspondent, but, when things were slow, he enjoyed ruining the reputation of gay clergymen, and exposing the marital difficulties of the elected. Basically, he was a rat. A filthy rodent that gnawed its existence off the flesh of those who deserved better than to fall on the pen of a shit like him, but they did. Real people made mistakes, and with Harry on hand, the Irish public could rest easy in the knowledge that those mistakes would get punished.

Jim Gilmore had made a mistake, according to Harry, as did Brian Furlong and Francis Hogan. In an article, published in the aftermath of the 1993 riots, Harry Ryan maintained that:

*Prison life is merely a reflection of society. In the public arena, we have the rich and the poor, the strong and the weak, the abuser and his victim. Behind the veil of secrecy that shrouds our penal institutions, we have no less a balance. We have the prison officers, undoubtedly rich from the fatted calf of cancerous overtime, empowered by the truncheon wielding escapades of their trade and abusive, it would seem, for no better reason than the barbaric nature of their condition. The prisoner, on the other hand, remains the victim of social ignorance. Made poor and weak by his stigma, the inmate is forced to claw his way down the grading ladder, to become the master of negativity.*

*What took place on the cold, grey rooftops of Meadowvale Prison on that damp August day, was the fall of tyranny to the hand of rebellion, a principle all too familiar to those of us still proud of our history.*

Afterwards, he visited The Percival Richards Bar And Tavern, to take comment from the jail enforcers who drank there, and got the bollox knocked out of himself for his troubles. They would pay for that one. Regardless of the eons they spent away from their families, regardless of the savage assaults, regardless of the stress and the strain and the occasional madness, Harry Ryan waged war on the wardens. Shortly after noon, he recieved a call to say that all hell had broken loose in Meadowvale, and that a media frenzy was about to take place. By the time the call had finished, he was in his car and he was barrelling dowm the motorway. By the time he arrived, there were cameras and cables, microphones and mobiles, and everywhere there was panic.

The prisoners would have to be locked up. For the moment, they were unaware of what was unfolding all around them. God forbid they should find out. That would only be a matter of time, but if the staff could remain calm long enough to feed the fuckers and bang out the cell doors, then they should be alright. By 12.30pm most of the jail was on lock down, and all available staff went to the blue wing. There were problems. Barry O Shea had decided to stage a sit down protest, and about a hundred or so prisoners were with him on the compound. Staff had pulled back, and although Paddy Devoy tried to placate them, the convicts would not budge and they screamed abuse and spat through the gates at the staff on the other side. At 1pm the unthinkable happened. A prisoner emerged from his cell, shouting at the others to calm down. When they did, he held up a radio. The one o clock news announcer gravely broadcast to the nation, that a child had been taken hostage by the notorious Sean Talbot, and that he was being held in a store room in Meadowvale Place Of Detention. The actual details were drowned out in the uproar that followed. Piss pots were emptied through the wire mesh onto staff, mattresses were set alight and everything that could be ripped or smashed off its hinges, was. On the other wings, inmates kicked at their doors and trashed their cells. The shit had well and truly hit the fan, and outside, reporters had to shout over the chaos to bring live link ups to the country.

Talbot sat with his back to the wall, facing the door. Conor sat between his legs, leaning into Talbots chest. A huge, muscled arm was strapped across his neck, and he was aware of the blade that rested against his cheek from time to time. The Beast talked incessantly, and every so often, he would hold the knife up to the door and he would use bad words. His voice was hoarse and his breath stank, but Conor was past caring. He had cried, bawled, called out for his father, pleaded with his captor and prayed to his maker, but all tono avail. He had given up, and there were moments when he thought it would be better if he were lying on the street by Devlins Corner, soaking up the wrath of the school delinquents. Talbot spoke to the door.

"Are yez listenin" he said and he rolled on the words as if he had to wade through them "I'll talk to de two bar"

The door seemed uncertain. "What was that you said?"

"I want de fuckin' Chief" screamed Talbot "I want de fucker now, or I'll cut dis little pricks head off, d'ya hear me?" and he scraped the weapon along Conors cheek. "Get de bastard, I said"

Augustine and Eileen sat in his office and squeezed the life from each other. The talking had stopped ages ago, it seemed, and the communicated now only with distress. The last time he had spoken, was to tell Sister Gertrude that he would see her burn in hell, before she ran through the baying journalists, and away. She told them, in passing, that she had no idea what was going on, and that she had only been in Meadowvale to deliver a message. Augustine dreaded the door handle. It would turn soon, he thought, and some harbinger of death would break the news to them of their sons demise. When it did turn, he closed his eyes and held his wife tighter than he had ever done before. Matty Morris stepped into the office.

"He's calling for you, Chief" he said

Augustine was on his feet. "Conor… Conor is calling for me" and Matty noticed that Mulcahys eyes were badly ravaged.

"No Chief" he said "Talbot. Talbot wants you. He says he'll speak to you" Eileens tortured face was dwarfed in his trembling hands, and when he kissed her, it was more an act of mercy than a gesture of love.

"I'll be back soon" he told her "and our boy will be with me"

When Bradford rolled into the tavern, he expected to be greeted with the usual festivity that accompanied the lunchtime rush. Normally the place was electric, but when Percy nodded at him, grimly, across the desolate space, he knew that some terrible deed had taken place. There was a spattering of strange faces at the counter, and a few seasoned scribes conversed with their Dictaphones, rattling off the bones off the next days editorial. It was a jail story, he gathered, and it wasn't good. Percival relayed the news, as he understood it, and the hacks filled in the rest. A cracking story, they told him, but then, one could always rely on the jailers to make headlines. There was no *genuine* concern in relation to the outcome of the ordeal, they merely wondered if 'the good ole boys' were on overtime for its duration. Shaw was disgusted with them. There was a child in there, at the hands of a madman, and the fine men and women of the service were in danger. Bridget was in there, as was Pablo and Doc and Dinny O Brien. They were decent and honest in a way that he understood, and it galled him to be in the company of these pen pushing mother fuckers, who knew nothing of them. He crashed through them like a bowling ball on his way out, and he made his way toward the jail.

When the door finally spoke to Talbot, it sounded just like a Chief. He was happy that it carried that stamp of authority, and he stated his demands.

"I want de key" he told it "I want de key to lock dis door. I don't trust youse fuckin' screw bastards, and when I gets uptight like dis, I'm liable to kill sometin" Augustine knew that if Conor was locked in with Talbot, he'd had it. 'The Beast' was capable of killing the boy at any moment and it would be detrimental to Conor if they tried to charge in, but they had to keep that option open. All Mulcahy wanted to do was to run in there and save his kid, but to attempt that now, would spell disaster. They would have to bide their time and negotiate. If an appropriate moment presented itself, they might be able to surprise the fucker. Talbot knew this also. That is why he wanted the key. After all, he would have to sleep sometime. It took a while, but the door responded.

"We never really use keys down here, Sean. It might take a bit of time to find it"

The voice sounded stressed, freaked out, on the edge. It needed some convincing. Talbot pulled Conors head back and dragged the blade across his throat. He opened his mouth and slithered his tongue across the boys skull. His voiced was torn and filled with malice.

"You got a little cunt for me... boy?"

Conor was confused. Mrs. Morrissey in the corner shop was 'a little cunt', his father had said so, but he there was no way he would be able to get her in here, not with someone like this.

Talbo roared at the door, so that everybody could hear.

"I SAID, HAVE YOU GOT A CUNT FOR ME... BOY?" and he tugged at the buttons on Conors trousers. The lad fought back. He scratched at Talbots hands and wriggled in his grip, but 'The Beast' grabbed him by the hair and smashed the butt of the knife against the side of his face. His head went numb and he slumped back. He was aware of Talbots hand, but was powerless to stop it. It fumbled into his underpants and cupped his scrotum. He could hear the Officers screaming and he identified his father, begging, pleading, but it would not stop. He felt his captor take a deep breath, and his eardrums exploded as 'The Beast' yelled out.

"I'm gonna rip his balls off and den I'm gonna fuck de hole. D'ya hear me, youse mother fuckers, I'm gonna fuck de hole"

Talbot squeezed, Conor squealed and he passed out.

Mulcahy was on the ground. His face was twisted and contorted, and his mouth was opened but no sound came out. He did not recall the stages of his sons life. He did not picture his face or remember his laugh. He knew only *that* moment. He had no knowledge of being helped to his feet, no memory of being held upright. He was aware only of the door, the door that separated him from his child, that divided him from his life, the door on the tomb of his soul. When he was led into the daylight, he was ignorant of Derek Gradys arm about him, remained untouched by his wifes despair and, in his fading, he knew little of what happened next.

Doc Grady stared blankly through the widow of the Chiefs office. Augustine was gone to them, broken so terribly, so... absolutely. Eileen was trying to hold onto him, but she was wilting herself. There was a terrible hurt that ran through them, a hurt that Doc knew well. He had woken up one morning following a binge. If he was to be honest, he had come to one afternoon following a proper fucking doozey... anyway, Jean had gone. She had been good enough to leave a letter by way of explanation, and she cited the booze and the fights and the withering dreams. He remembered that pain, that hurt. He remembered the awful lonliness and the regret. He remembered. Talbot had a child down there, just a fucking kid. A kid who would never get the chance to be happy, never get the opportunity to fall in love. Doc had been happy, *he* had fallen in love. He had lost it, sure, but it was there once. When he had lived without her, he thought that he would die. In a way, he did. He never wanted to go back to that, to the darkness, but there were no guarantees. Jean was back, but for how long? A day, a week, forever... *never*. He could walk home to an empty room later, who knows? No... there was a young boy down there with his whole life ahead of him. He might never make the mistakes that Doc had made, he could be... *happy*. He certainly deserved the chance to find out. He was going to get it. Doc went to the keys office and located the store room bunch. He ambled outside and stared up at the clouds.

"Jesus it's hot" he said and pulled at his collar. The rain ran like treacle on his neck "Fucking Irish weather, I certainly wont miss you" and he sauntered down into the pit.

(iv)   SO LONG FRIEND

The jailhouse smelled like a shithouse which, to those familiar with such places, meant that it smelled just like a jailhouse. Foul gloups of human faeces floated on billabongs of piss, and the smoke from smouldering mattresses swirled out through cell doors and formed a thick black cloud that blocked off the upper tiers. But, it was not the smoke or the shit or, indeed, the piss that concerned the staff, it was the mob. The mob was armed and dangerous, sent delirious with rage and turned savage by its hatred. They brandished knives, iron bars, raw clumps of steel and blood filled syringes. Their fury demanded a battle. They taunted the Officers, invited the fight and their threats were made personal. Wives would be raped, children defiled, houses burned and all around, the symphony of destruction drifted through the din and danced about the ears of the good folk of Meadowvale. But, they could not be touched by the mob, nor scarred by it, nor moved, for this was their place and when the time was right, they would have it back. Until then, they waited, waited and stood together, for behind the debauchery and the depression and the fucked up dreams, there was a dedication to one another that would see them charge foolhardy into the face of uncertainty. If that's what it took, then so be it, and if Sister Gertrude wondered what kind of man or woman stands in a jailers shoes, her answer stood shoulder to shoulder in the circle of Meadowvale Prison, if only she had bothered to stay around long enough to find out.

It was never Denis O Briens intention to ease the pains of Sean Talbot. After all, he had taken away the heart of Dinny, the very soul of him. In 1993, Talbot had half kicked the life from Jim Gilmore, before throwing him from the roof. A twisted, sordid little bastard like that, had stolen the life of a friend, a brother, a soul mate. What a tough guy, to beat up an old man on the bleak, grey roof top, and then to hurl him over the edge a hundred feet to the ground. Sean the jail hero, Sean the hard man, Sean the sick fuck. Young boys and old men, that's some C.V for sure. But Dinny was an old pro. No point in being honest at a time like this. He spoke softly and his voice was calm and precise.

"Sean" he said quietly "how are you bearing up in there? You've got to talk to us, son, otherwise we can't help you. Is there anything you need, anything that we can get for you?"

But Sean did not want to talk. Sean wanted to play, and he had just the ticket. Conor Mulcahy was coming round and his head lolled from side to side on Talbots groin. His sense of reality was hazy, at best, and along with the blurred images and the nausea, there were strange tones that made demands of him. A voice from the dark side urged him to open his mouth, *wider, wider, wider,* and in his dreamlike state, he complied. By the time he had fully opened his eyes, the beast was kneeling over him. He had his trousers opened and he held in his hand something that looked like a willy, the biggest willy that Conor had ever seen, like a torpedo maybe or a space rocket. The bad man wanted to put the thing into his mouth, for some reason, but Conor wouldn't have it. He tried to break free. He slapped and kicked and punched and cried out, but the bad man grabbed his face and squeezed his jaws until his lips parted. The rocket jabbed at his cheeks and pushed his nose sideways. It was hot and slimy and it smelled of something much worse than wee. He struggled for all he was worth, but the man was strong and his hands were locked on the boys face so tightly that Conor thought that his skull would burst. The willy thrust deep into his throat and he gagged. Then, his whole head was pulled up by the hair and slammed back down, and up by the hair and down again and again and again, and he stopped fighting it, gave in to it... died to it. When his mouth filled up and 'The Beast' roared out, Conor puked, or at least his body did. *He* had stopped caring. There were voices outside that called his name, but he was not with them now, he was far away. Talbot turned him over without a skirmish, and a soothing breeze caressed his buttocks as they were laid bare. The mans threats did not frighten him anymore, and the promise that his hole would be busted meant little to him. Talbot leaned forward to penetrate, but before he did, the door spoke to him and its voice was that of Doc Gradys.

When Bradford Shaw arrived at the prison gates, the place was transformed. Throngs of people had gathered, and amidst the cameras and the microphones and the media personnel, jailers families huddled in the rain and waited on news from the front. There was very little *actual* information coming out, and the rumour machine was in overdrive. A warden had been set on fire, prisoners had broken into the segregation unit and paedophiles were being murdered, the child was dead and there were stories of cowardice and tales of bravery that were noted and quoted for lusty editors the length and breadth of Ireland. Shaw did not feel out of place in any way. He had a right to be there. The men beyond those gates had shone a light into the void of his spirit, and he proudly wore the bruises of his bout with Bridget. A rosary was underway and, though he would mumble through, at best, he bowed his head and joined in.

Dinny O Brien and the others were crying when Doc arrived. They could not speak and they did not wish to do so ever again. Their faces were trapped in the horror of the moment and their hearts were ripped asunder by 'The Beast'. This had gone on for far too long. Doc marched past them and banged on the store room door. He carried a conviction about him that was reminiscent of the old Doc, the Derek Grady before the fall.

"Sean Talbot" he said "this is Officer Grady. The media are outside, the newspapers, the radio stations, the T.V networks, the whole fucking circus. Right now, we are live into every home in the country. Your family are watching, Sean, along with every filthy creature you ever knew, and here you are, holding a child hostage. How is that going to look, do you think? Sean Talbot, the beast of little boys... you yellow fucking snake. Why don't you let the kid go and take me instead. The world will understand it if you take a jailer. They will say that we beat you, that we tortured you for the riot. They will say that we had it coming, Sean, and you'll be a hero all over again, just like '93. So what do you say mother fucker? Do you fancy your chances with a big boy or are you really just the snivelling prick I always said you were. This is your chance to go down as the main man, Seanie Fuckpig. It's your call. I have the key to this door in my pocket, we can lock ourselves in and have ourselves a party. Now,

you've got ten seconds and then I walk out those gates and I tell mammy and daddy Talbot just what a useless bastard they brought into the world" and he began counting.

Dinny was all over him. This was suicide and the big fella knew it.

"What the fuck are you at" he said "That psychopath is going to cut you to pieces"

But Doc did not care.

"Three, four, five" he was screaming.

"Jesus Christ, man, you have your whole fucking life ahead of you"

"Six, seven" "Doc" Dinny pleaded "Doc, are you listening to me?"

But he was not. He was listening only to heart.

"Eight, nine, ten. Okay shit for brains, what's it to be?"

Dinny was in his face now, begging him.

"Stop this. You've got a second chance. A chance to things right this time. Go home to Jean, Doc, please, for the friendship that we've had, please, Doc, stop this now"

But it was too late. The door was pulled open, and they were treated to the sight of Sean Talbot, furious with rage, holding a knife to the throat of a blank faced waif who was naked from the waist down.

"Alright" said 'The Beast' "Whichever one of youse dat was, step into de room and push de door closed. I'll let de swine go and we'll start again. And I'm gonna make yez fuckin' pay yez bastards"

Dinny stared at Doc and Doc stared back. This was it. So long friend, thanks for everything. Both men stood in each others gaze, and there was a smile between them, a last smile for happier times, before Derek Grady stepped forward. He was about to breach the threshold, when a mighty hand grabbed him and pulled him close. Denis O Brien pressed his face against Docs and whispered

"For a friend, Doc, for a friend" and he knocked Derek to safety as he slipped inside the lair, closing the door behind him.

Shortly after, Conor Mulcahy burst into the hallway and ran down the tunnel toward the light. He was screaming all the way. Meanwhile inside, Dinny was dragged to the floor, where he suffered the backlash of Docs great speech.

(v)　　WHAT WILL BE, WILL BE

It had turned out to be such a bad day for everyone, and that included Nora Hegarty. She had gone to the well too many times and age was not on her side anymore. She was battered with exhaustion, but still, she had found herself pacing the floor in the early hours. She had looked in on Sean far more often than was necessary, feeling, perhaps, that he would be gone from her soon. When he slept, it was easy to remember him as he had been and when she ran her fingers through his hair in the stillness, Nora wept for things that could never be. Victor arrived, as usual, at eight to administer the Bupivicaine, but Nora sat him at the kitchen table and held his hands.

"It's over" she said and her voice was broken with the heartache "What will be, will be. We're not going to find anyone who is willing to have him, at this stage, and if David Orr is going to take him from me on Thursday, I don't want to see Sean suffer any longer. No more needles, Victor, I want him back"

He put his arms around her and she shared her tears.

"Okay" he said "No more needles. It's going to be a while before the medication of the past few days wears off, but when it does, everything will be as it was. There's still a few days, and God is good. Who knows what might happen" but he did not believe that anymore, he didn't believe any of it.

    By midday, the news of the Jail was everywhere. Victor got wind of it when he ventured out to pick up the Sunday papers and he rushed back to let her know. They were devastated. The warders were a good crew and they had always been respectful to the locals. Sure, they were mad bastards most often, but then, the people of the village had seen first hand what they had to contend with. When the place exploded in 1993, the townsfolk were shocked at the violence and when the three lads were killed, it left a hollow feeling in everyone that would not go away. Victor had prepared the bodies for burial and the beating that those men had sustained was grotesque. In the days since then, the town had been plagued with petty crime. Prisoners families would come to visit them and shop items would be lifted, car windows would get smashed and sometimes, used syringes would be found in laneways or in the school yard. What existed inside the prison walls was worse. The amount of times they had seen the jailers battered up was sinful, and no one could understand how those poor bastards worked every day of every week, forever. The papers would regularly print articles about the overtime as if the warders had created it, but that was just a barefaced lie and if the boys and girls of the prison enjoyed the high roller life of the jet set, then they sure as hell didn't show it.

They forgot about their troubles for a short time and, as soon as Sean was in his chair, they went to the jail to where the others had gathered. It was hard to believe that this shit was happening again. Surely changes would have been made after the first time, and what, exactly, was the idea of bringing that awful man back to Meadowvale. Good Lord, will they never learn. Sometime after two o clock, an ambulance rushed through the gates and the gardai arrived in numbers. Apparently, the child had been freed in exchange for a warder, but no name was given. There was a clatter of cameras and the twist was broadcast to the nation. In the melee, Nora spotted Bradford Shaw and recognised him as the jailers new friend from the tavern. He looked terrible and the ordeal of manoeuvring his way about the press corp was talking its toll. She helped him to one side and asked if there was anything she could do for him.

"No ma'am" he said in his southern drawl "I'm doing just fine. You have your hands full anyway" and he nodded to Sean "How's the young man bearing up"

"It's very kind of you to ask" she said "He's a fighter"

Bradford leaned across and tapped Sean on the shoulder.

"Fighters got to stick together" he said and he held out his hand.

Sean rocked from side to side and his eyes drifted from Shaws.

"He doesn't talk" said Nora, and she introduced herself and her son.

"A great pleasure to make your acquaintance, ma'am" and he was polite enough to offer his name. "Will you be attending the prayer meeting tomorrow evening?"

"Oh, you haven't heard" and she sounded surprised "The meeting has been brought forward to tonight. The group will be praying for the safe return of the officer, I suppose. It's the least we can do"

"Of course it is, yes. Well I suppose I'll see you there then" said Shaw "I have to go and eat. I've been here for some time. I hope we can expect miracles tonight, we're going to need them"

Nora stared at Sean. "We are indeed" she said "We are indeed"

Jean Cooke had gone back to bed when Doc left for work. She had not slept well the previous night. Derek Grady was still a haunted man and he tossed and turned into the wee hours, troubled and unsettled. She did not wake again till after three, but she was tired. She sat on the sofa and sipped black coffee. There seemed like a million issues to resolve and she wondered if, deep in her soul, she had the want or the strength to face them all. It would be so easy just to walk away. Right this minute, she could open the door and take to the hills. She could put one foot in front of the other and on and on into the distance, no more heartache, no more tears. But that was it, you see, there *would* be heartache and there *would* be tears and sadness and loneliness, because there had been ever since she had left. She loved Doc Grady, every last inch of him, and so lay her dilemma. Her head was hurting now and she thought that she might just deal with this later. She turned on the radio in the hope of finding a soothing tune, and she got the news.

Veronica Gilmore was already at the jail, when she arrived. The place was like a war zone and in the thick of the battle, Percival Richards was handing out flyers to the ever growing troupe. Veronica brought her up to date on the events.

"They wont give out the name of the Officer" she cried "They say it's for security reasons. For Christs sake, he's already a hostage. How much more insecure can he be. I know it's Dinny, Jean, I just know it." And she burst into tears.

"Don't be worried. Today's his last day. He's probably in the tea cabin waiting for news just like us"

But Veronica would not be consoled. "There are issues that he's wanted to address since '93, a guilt that he's carried, the silly old fool, and I *know* him, Jean, I know him too well"

"Have you asked the lads on the gate? Surely they know what's going on"

"I'm too afraid" said Veronica "What would I do without him? I can't do this again"

But Jean was afraid also. Doc could be in there, now, this minute, with 'The Beast' and there not a thing she could do to save him. Same old story. While she was hoping, Veronica made her way through the crowd and tapped on the main gate of Meadowvale Jail. Pablo Rogers stared at her blankly and whispered the words "I'm sorry", and when she collapsed, Jean held her tight, while bulbs flashed and news cameras walloped against each other in a bid to film the anguish.

Augustine Mulcahy could not console his son. Had the boy been crying, he could have eased his pain with soft words, but he shed no tears nor did he return their gaze. He seemed unaware of their presence, and when he had stopped screaming, he just stopped, like an old clock. Mulcahy noticed that Conor was guarding his genitals beneath the blanket, and he closed his eyes, afraid to ask. But his tone was warm and composed, in so much as it could be.

"Did he hurt you, son... touch you... I mean?"

He caught a tremble on the boys lips and a single teardrop ran the length of his flushed cheek. He tried to speak, but each time the words would fall away somewhere inside of him, and when they did come, they brought with them the anger and the pain, the pity and the shock and the devastating horror of his ordeal.

"IN MY MOUTH" he bawled, and his fingers quivered as they pointed to his ravaged face, while his eyes burned into Augustines, pleading for mercy, roaring for compassion as if they would be glazed forever with the image of 'The Beast' and beastly things.

Mulcahy carried his son to the ambulance and placed him on the stretcher. He would not allow anyone to touch him and it was only when Eileen was with him, that he let him go. They raced through the gates and away. There was nothing that the jail could take from him now, nothing left to lose, and he *would* see this through. He *would* have his moment. He went to his office and, as he steadied himself for the fight, he caught his reflection.

"Right" he muttered "it's time to find out who you *really* are... horse" then he turned and headed out.

It was well past 5pm and Chief Officer Augustine Mulcahy walked into the circle, where he resumed control.

(vi)   **HOLDING BACK THE YEARS**

Sean Talbot was worn out from the beating that he had given to the old warder. His fists were swollen and the knife handle had become pasty with several layers of congealed blood. A foul looking gash decorated the length of Dinnys face and he was aware of the warm flow that ran, constantly, from his nose and his mouth. There seemed to be a hectic movement outside. Several times, the door would creak open and he would catch sight of their faces, but, each time, Talbot would drive the knife tip into Dinny and the door would be hastily closed. He could hear them, bargaining frantically, but if they could see the bastards face, they would have known that he had absolutely no interest in give and take. So he just lay there and he stared past the cob webbed ceiling, past the dark, apocalyptic clouds to the heavens and to Jim, where he asked his old friend for one last favour.

"If you can help me, Jim" he whispered and he tapered off "You know yourself"

Negotiations were one sided and, eventually, things went quiet. Thunder rumbled outside and the swelter made him fade. He succumbed to the calling of his own past, and Denis O Brien drifted.

1974: He was happy. Age had not yet withered him and he was young and handsome and lean. In a bar whose name had long since vanished, the king was still the king and, as a well thumbed juke box rocked and rolled, they be bopped and jive hopped to therebel sounds of their youth. Jim Gilmore was there, larger than life, and so was *she*. My God, had he really managed to suppress her in his old age? He knew, of course, that he had not, indeed he could not, for a return to that day, perhaps his happiest, was a return to her and he would never separate them, not for time, not for wisdom, not for peace. She was the last great relic of the life he had once known and when that innocence passed, the world, *his* world, was a darker place for it. But that would come later. For one moment in history, they danced and sang... and loved absolutely. They punched the air. They were alive.

1978: She was gone, had enough. He had changed, she said, and although she still felt a fondness for him, she did not love him that way anymore. He had become jail rough and not... *nice*... like he had been. The place was inside him now, eating away at his spirit, and the piss pots and the shit parcels had knocked it out of him. He had lost the boy in him, she lamented, the boy that she had cared for so deeply. He sat in the shadows with the whiskey, and punched the walls. It was over.

1984: Jim and Veronica raised their glasses to him, and they toasted in a brand new year. The party was too hectic and he found himself trading stouts with a rookie, all nervous and respectful. A nice kid, young Derek, a little naïve perhaps but who hadn't been. Dinny wished him well and offered him his counsel should he ever need it. Jim made the announcement, named the big day, and he missed her more than ever. He wondered if she thought of him sometimes, if, perhaps, he might not see her again, and he allowed himself the pleasure of dreaming, just a little. But, before the night was over, he would be broken. A warder from Dublin, who understood that Dinny would surely have known by then, broke the news to him. There had been car crash, some years earlier, on the outskirts of the city and she had not survived the collision. It happened in the Autumn of 1980 and, having met them on occasion at Prison get togethers, the warden recognised her photograph in the paper. He was sorry for Dinnys troubles and he left him to grieve... and he certainly did that.

How could he not have known. But, then again, how could he have. When she left, she left for good and his attempts to trace her were futile. He would have pleaded with her, he thought, shown her the change in him, made her understand, but that was gone too. Happy new year. It punched through his soul.

1993: He was wretched. Time had not healed his wound and he cursed the fuckers for telling him that it would. Another bus had not come along and if there were plenty more fish in the sea, he would let the sharks have them. He had been a regular visitor to the therapy counter and, that day, he was drunk. When the news came in, he rushed back to the jail. He could hear them on the roof, goading and taunting. The men looked to him. He had trained most of them and he was their leader. He fumbled his way into a riot suit and made his way to the ladders. He was loose and Jim knew. He must have. He had carried Dinny for weeks, and when he had left him in the pub earlier, he was all talked out. He stepped in and took Dinnys place. It seemed like the right thing to do.

The last man up was Brian Furlong. He remembered him again, his peach fuzz cheeks stretched in a great country mans smile, as he climbed to the fight, waving to Dinny, waving goodbye. It was never about the place, or the job, it was about the loyalty. When he saw them laid out later, they were battered, busted and still. He sat with them alone until the hearses came, and while they were loaded up, he punched out.

There were faces greeting him now, in the silence of an old prison store room. She floated from the dim light and she was as radiant as she had always been. Her blonde curls danced along the shoulders of her red dress and her pale blue eyes sparkled in the gloom. And Jim was there, calling the horse to pasture, and Brian, and there were others from a time so distant that he had forgotten. He thought of Veronica, good, sweet, decent Veronica. He did love her, he thought, because she reminded him of a time when they were both happy… with someone else. He opened his eyes and the faces were gone, yet, for all of the serenity that they had granted him, he was afraid, so terribly afraid. He did not want to die, not here, not like this. Night settled in on them, and beyond the tomb door, weary men would battle for his soul and their own lives.

(vii)   **TOUCHED BY AN ANGEL**

The holy road was a lonely place. Set outside of the village, in the heartland of rural Ireland, it drew crowds only on prayer night and, more often than not, it was a spectacle merely for cattle and stray sheep. The hey day of the pilgrimage had seen vast congregations in pious adoration. They would travel across the globe, and descend on the place in horse drawn carriages and jaunting carts. The town had boomed from the custom. By the time the first motor car spluttered through the town, things had become somewhat slower. The lure of Fatima was strong and Lourdes was producing the goods in a way that Meadowvale was not. Years later, Christ was appearing on oatmeal biscuits and statues of the Virgin Mary were tap dancing for live audiences in sleepy hollows everywhere. The arse had fallen out of the pilgrim market and Meadowvale was just another casualty. There had been a steady, but weak, trade, lifted only when Boss Keane had his good fortune and that had lasted just about long enough to hit the local papers. Those who attended this wet and stormy Sunday night, expected little but hoped for much. Such was the way of the trail.

All of the ailments were represented, and along with the crippled and the maimed, there were those who sought redemption. There was Lively Lilly Mac, who could have sucked the chrome off a trailer hitch in her day, and there were the local hairdressers Paddy Whack and Cecil B, who had been cursed with the homosexuality for robbing Vincent de Paul boxes when they were at school. Podge Horan had developed a genital mutation, he believed, from self abuse and Alison Finch had begun sprouting horny protrusions from her forehead following her support for the pro-abortion campaign. It was a wonder that the jailers had not morphed for their sins. Perhaps the almighty felt that they had enough on their plate, who knows. The novena was about to begin, and, in a scene lifted straight from 'Zombie Holocaust', the wounded and the afflicted, the twisted and the torn, descended on a bleak country by-road in search of the divine. Brad Shaw was among them.

Mulcahy was concerned for Doc Grady. For as long as he had known him, Derek had been out there, on the edge. Now, with the monstrous upheaval in full swing, he was showing signs of wear, and the pressure was visible for all to see. Augustine would understand Docs reluctance to leave, but he insisted on it.

"Leave the jail, Derek" he said "Go for a walk, clear your head, and when you're ready to come back, all this shit will still be here"

A walk… yes, to clear his head… yes. Maybe he could, for just a few minutes. This could last all night, or all week even, nobody knew. The night air would help. It would freshen his resolve, make it strong. He would need his strength for Dinny, they all would. The Chief would rotate everyone throughout the ordeal, give them all a chance for some respite. They were to leave by the back door, no journalists. Doc was the first man out. He was mush. His brain was melted and needed the therapy. He needed it real bad. The tavern was calling and he would not be impolite. Just this one time, he told himself, just this once and that would be it.

Jean Cooke, Veronica Gilmore and the others were ushered into a side room by the main gate. They were away from the cameras, at least, and that was something. There was no update on the situation and the longer they waited, the worse things appeared. They drank strong coffee and occasionally they prayed. They said a decade at about ten thirty, and when they were finished, Veronica burst into tears and said that Jim was waiting for Dinny... waiting to take him home.

By eleven, the big guns were in. All the way from the penthouse suites of their Galway H.Q, the smoked salmon socialists of The Jail Wardens Union, the JWU, looked concerned, talked the talk and held the high moral ground. They were not the official association, but they represented the disgruntled members of Meadowvale. President of the organisation, Muiris O Toole, had been in bed with the officials so often that he was known as 'The Whore'. He had not actually been to the prison in such a long time, that he would have driven past the place, had it not been for the growing crowds outside it. Never one to avoid the media, he waved to the cameras as he went in. He swaggered, now, throughout the staff and appealed for calm. Meantime, in the real world, serious people dealt with serious shit as only *they* knew how.

Brad Shaw spotted the Hegartys in the crowd and made his way to them. They were located in the section marked miscellaneous and, as he approached, Shaw saw that they were surrounded by a weird and wonderful assembly of the *'not quite right'*. There were men with gammy legs that twitched independently and women with crooked eyes, that would, without co-operation, stare at you intensely, before wandering off to focus on another.

A small group that suffered from Turret Syndrome, held hands and called out for mercy.

"FUCK, SHIT and praise you Jesus"

All in all, it was not a bad crowd, and the organisers were heard to say that such volume had not been seen in Meadowvale since the 'Rolling Stones' tribute band, Jumpin' Jack cacks, had played a benefit gig to replace Rasher Murphys burnt out caravan in 1994.

Nora was leaning over Sean, combing his hair, while Victor Roberts was murdering the end of a cigarette and struggling to hold his trousers at a respectable level above his builders crack. They seemed glad to see him. Nora helped him in beside Sean, and she laid her hand on his shoulder as things got underway. She was a sad lady, he thought, and he felt compelled to tap her hand reassuringly for reasons he could not explain. She was in deep prayer.

"Lord" she whispered "why have you abandoned me? I have been devoted to you... all my life. I have had few comforts, as you know, but if he is taken from me, I *will* die. I don't know why the accident happened, that was your call, but I accepted your will. Now, I beg of you sweet Jesus, be with me on this. I need to know that you still have pity on us" and the tears rolled freely "Show me that you haven't forgotten us, Lord... please. Give me something... anything" As the desperation ran through her fingers and saw them tighten on Shaw, a voice called out her name. It was Doc Grady.

The sing song was in full flow. Dinny could not remember when he had laughed so hard and he threw pints on the counter in the hope that it might last forever. Veronica told him that he was working too hard, and he was about to answer, when Jim took her hand and led her to the dance.

"Sorry, old son" he said "but I think that you're already spoken for" and he was.

She was with him, just like she had been all those years ago. So beautiful, just so beautiful, and as they waltzed, he could feel the years fade away. He was that guy again. That other guy, who was untouched by the hurt... unspoiled. Doc floated past.

"You're a damned attractive man, Denis" he quipped "Don't think that I haven't noticed" and they laughed harder than ever. Even when Jean dragged him away and told him not to be making such a fool of himself, Doc was cracking jokes, till she gave in to it and fell about with them. The tempo picked up and Dinny found himself on a head to head with Jim Gilmore for King of the dance floor. They rattled and rolled and kicked up their heels. The crowd cheered them on and the music and the drink had him swirling. Jim leaned in and tapped his cheek. For some reason he was telling him to wake up. The taps became slaps and Jim was shouting now.

"Wake up, wake up" and he opened his eyes in time to see Talbots open palm rushing toward him.

"WAKE UP YEZ FUCKIN' SCUMBAG" and the blow was numbing when it landed.

"Ah, there youse are" said 'The Beast' "How de hell are yez. I tought dat I'd lost ye dere for a second" and he whispered to Dinny "Not just yet. But soon now... very soon"

Nora was surprised to see Doc. With all that was happening in the jail, he was the last person she expected to see. They were full of questions. How was it going. Was anybody hurt. Would things be alright. But Doc was hurried and he wanted to get back.

"I was on my way to... a place" he said "A place I thought I needed to go. But when I put my hand in my pocket, I found these" and he produced Magners letters "and I remembered that I had something far more important to do. I called to the guesthouse but there was no one home and then I was told that you'd be here. Can you sit down. I think you'll need to" and he explained everything. She could not believe it. How could they. The bastards. How could they have put them through all this... for a fucking house. But could he prove it. Was he sure.

"You leave that to me" he said "I know what to do. But I must ask you for a favour"

"Anything"

"Do *not* call the gardai. I know that it seems like the right thing to do, and it is, but there's something else that I need to sort out and if you do as I ask, some good may come from all this" He spoke to Bradford Shaw. "You may be staying with us after all, my friend" and with that, he was gone. There were still unresolved issues in the jail.

The whole prison had gone berserk. It was almost impossible to accept that human beings could be so savage, so barbaric. But they were. They were like animals and they charged at the partitions, with their faces covered, and chucked pots of fresh urine at the staff. They called them on. Screamed, shrieked and lusted for blood, craved the unthinkable. The staff were exhausted and some of them wandered out, occasionally, to escape the butchery.

Tony Ennis stood on the steps that led into the prison, and hocked up a thick black sputum.

"Jesus Christ" he said "What the fuck is that"

Gardai and Army had arrived throughout the evening. They surveyed the building, climbed onto vantage points, drew diagrams, consulted with each other and decided that, all things considered, they had absolutely no idea what they were at. Peter O Driscoll approached Tony and, by way of explanation, he said that the lads were only doing a job.

"Aren't we all" said Ennis "Aren't we all"

Mulcahy wondered how there were so many breakables in a place that was supposed to operate on basics. At this stage, convicts were just smashing things into smaller pieces, and another problem had reared its head. In the euphoria of the riot, the Blue wing inmates had partied hard and just about all of the smack was in their arms by tea time. Now at 1am on Monday morning, it was starting to dawn on them that the party was over. No more good shit for the boys. In an ideal world, one of them would have come forward with moderate demands, promises would have been given and some accommodation would have been reached. But in reality, principles and prisoners often mix badly, and without a functioning brain between them, the train rolled on.

Augustine did not give a shit. He paced up and down with the phone to his ear.

"Governor" he barked "where in the fuck have you been?"

Delahunty would not have it and he told him so. He would have him sacked for insubordination if need be.

"Oh, yeah" said Mulcahy "not before I kick ten kinds of shit out of you first, you horrible little prick. If the department find out that you were warned about this in advance, it will be your miserable fucking ass nailed to the mast. So keep your mouth shut and I'll decide what to do with you later" and he hopped the phone off the wall.

Murtagh Delahunty inched his way up from the back seat of his car and stared out the window. From the Officers car park, he could see the circus outside the Jail. He inched back down again.

"Fuck" he said "fuck, fuck, fuck"

It did not appear that any major breakthrough was about to happen inside the jail, and word had gone round the journalists about the prayer group. Harry Ryan decided that it would be no harm to get a few photos for the roundups, so he headed out to the holy road for the craic. A cack handed hack from the big smoke like Ryan, would only delight at the opportunity to poke fun at the misguided devotions of 'the culchies and the zealots' who prayed for the safe passage of the hard knuckled turn keys of the jail. To him, they were ignorant rural folk who had not yet discovered modern medicine. In reality, they had exhausted it, and that many of them were praying for men and women they did not know, was only an indication of his own ignorance. He slithered through the crowd, noting ailments as he went.

Brad Shaw was mulling over Docs comment. What had he meant, he might be staying after all. He had explained to Grady that he could not afford the land and that had not changed. He was having difficulty concentrating. The choir was loud and the congregation clapped and swayed to a beat. He was desperately trying to address the issue, when he saw something that rocked him to his roots. It could not be, he told himself, it was a trick of the light. But it wasn't and he knew it. The guy beside him, the Sean Hegarty fellow, the *cripple*, was... ... tapping his feet.

"Jesus holy Christ" he exclaimed and he drew attention. People in the section gathered round and gasped. But Sean was oblivious. All he knew was the rhythm and he could feel it now, in his heart, in his soul, in his legs. It was taking him and he wanted to go... so he did.

To the shock of those around him, Sean Hegarty whipped off his blanket and threw himself into the air, into freedom. As the cameras snapped and Harry Ryan almost choked himself with his lanyard, Nora Hegarty laughed and cried and called out all at once. Her son was back, back to stay. She reached out and touched him through the throng, and when the words finally left him and he called out "Maaamaaa", they laughed and cried together.

It was all too much for Shaw. There was a powerful surge through his body and he felt himself shudder. It was blackening. He was dizzy with it, drunk by it, and he could feel the blood course through his own legs, like he had been touched by an angel. As Sean Hegarty threw his limbs at the Meadowvale sky, Shaw felt a series of jolts through both thighs and, before he had the chance to contemplate it, he was on his feet. He was unsteady, but he was up and he would stay up. There was a rapturous applause from the group and shouts of "BOLLOX" and "SHITEBAGS" from the Turrets, who clapped harder than any.

A few others threw down their crutches and keeled over, and one woman claimed she'd been fondled, but it was the greatest night for many a long year, and with the media on hand to capture it all, Meadowvale was back in business.

(viii)   THE LAST ALONE

The voices beyond the door were unfamiliar to Dinny, and there was a desperation about them that suggested they were, most probably, gardai. As the night had forged ahead, people came and went, and with each passing hour, hopes of a resolution seemed to fade. Negotiations were in disarray. Talbot had what he wanted and he paid little heed to the offers of leniency on display. What was there for him, but a lifetime of captivity. The filthy jailers had seen to that. He remembered them taking the stand and sending him down the line. The bastards sowed him up for the judge, and he would spend the next ten years pissing into a pot for his troubles. Did they really think that he would just lie down for them? Was it their understanding that the beast in him would give up like some sick puppy?

They were *always* going to pay, it was only a matter of opportunity. The shit he had to endure in convincing those holy Joe mother fuckers, that he was a changed man, that he had seen the error of his ways, that a return to this place would *"help the recovery, sir"*. All those crocodile tears into the handkerchiefs of watery eyed women, all those soul baring sessions with college boys and weak old men. But it worked. Here he was, king of the fucking world, and if they thought that he had given them something to write about in 1993, they would want to start sharpening their pencils. The best was yet to come.

Matty Morris had given the Chief an update and was on his way back to the bunker, when he met Pablo Rodgers. Paul had manned the main gate throughout the evening and he had missed the fine details of the ordeal. There was no change. Things did not look good but they kept on trying. Doc was in the tunnel when they arrived. They were no strangers to hard nights, but they had come to an impasse on this one and they were running awful short on bright ideas. If Dinny was to take another beating, it would kill him. That much they were sure of. Even if they could get him out now, there were no guarantees that he would pull through. The last time food was delivered, the floor was drenched in blood, and they doubted any of it was Talbots. Should they charge in, it could spell the end for the big guy. 'The Beast' had the shank to Dinnys throat, and regardless of how groggy the day had left Talbot, speed would not be on their side.

"He's not giving up, lads" said Pablo "He's here to hurt" and by that he meant "kill", he just couldn't say it.

"Alright then" said Doc "We *are* in agreement. If this doesn't finish soon, the fucker will finish him" He couldn't say it either.

"So, what do we do now?" said Matty.

Doc Grady closed his eyes. The decision terrified him.

"We go in" he said, and they looked pitiful to each other in the dark.

Denis O Brien lay cradled against Sean Talbot amidst the store room boxes. Were it not for the knife, they could have been war wounded buddies on the Somme, but allies they were not. They were, both of them, forged by events from another age. A day long gone that was, in some respects, the last day of what they were, of the men they used to be, and, finding themselves here together, was an opportunity to balance the books. Talbot did not know Dinny. He didn't know what he had taken from him, didn't know what he had left with him. But Dinny knew. He knew plenty, and in the stillest hours of his darkest night, he found a strength that he thought was gone. It came from the guilt and the sadness, from the long years and the old days. It came from Jim and Francis Hogan and from Furlongs great smile. And it came, now, to Denis O Brien, father to a jailer generation, in the wee small hours of his retirement.

Talbot was hurling abuse at the others, when he was startled by the sound of his own name. He had taken it that the old warder was done for, but, when Dinny spoke to him like that, he was caught off guard. He did not expect it when he was told that *his* time had come, and he was shocked to his shit heeled shoes when the big, grey guy drove his skull upwards and into Talbots face. His nose burst on impact and, in the blind pain that consumed him, he was unable to prevent the assailant from locking his head. They tussled. Both men were aware of the staffs efforts to get into the room, but in the fracas, they had rolled behind the door and it made things difficult. They were alone in there. Dinny could feel the white hot intrusions of the blade into his chest and his gullet, and he strangled 'The Beast' with such force that he rocked to and fro upon the resistance of Talbots neck beneath him. His fingers were armour plated as they twisted and crushed, and though he was aware of the steel ripping at his flesh, he was numb to it. A horrible sound filled the night as the last gasps of the convict became a dying mans song. Dinny was rabid, out of control. He pounded Talbot against the drenched tiles, and he throttled 'The Beast' till his strength gave way to fate. A terrible darkness overcame him and he slumped forward. It was over.

The door burst open and they rushed in. Denis O Brien and Sean Talbot were stretched out on the store room floor beside each other. The business of vengeance had been a messy one, and Officers skated and slipped on the residue of that nights work. Talbots face was contorted. His eyes reached out and his tongue was lathered as if he had been put to sleep. His purple complexion would rule out an open casket and he had soiled himself in the moments after death. An unremarkable trickle of blood leaked from his nostrils and meandered along his cheek. Dinny was not so lucky. He was covered in it. The shirt that he had pressed for his last jail day was ripped and torn, and a battery of ugly, gaping wounds peeped out from beneath. He was punctured everywhere. The face that had reassured them on a thousand long shifts was gone and the mask that disguised it was swollen and hurted and pale. Doc Grady cradled his old friend and cried out to no one in particular.

(ix)   TAKE IT BACK

Sooner or later they would have given up. They'd have gotten hungry or bored or pissed off. What the hell, prisoners did it all the time, let off a little steam. They might empty a bucket of shit on a screw or bust him up with a cue ball or stab the fucker with a needle. So what, big fucking deal. They would spend a few evenings behind doors, miss a movie or two. Boo… fucking… hoo. *But not tonight.* If the system wanted to bend over and take it up the tea towel holder, then such is life, but not tonight.

Augustine Mulcahy sat in his office and stared at his hands. Whose hands were they? Centuries ago, they clawed the air and grabbed at the cane. They clasped together and begged for it to stop. They were a victims hands.

Later, they would reach out to greet the bastard Governor, with the promise that they would deliver the heads of men he did not know, decent men who covered up their own scars. They were dirty, filthy hatchet mans hands.

And, of course, they were thieves hand. He had forgotten about that. There, in the drawer… stolen money. Stolen fucking money with these rotten fucking hands.

But earlier, much, much earlier, they were almost the hands of a good man, almost. They held them close to him at breakfast, felt the warmth of their bodies, of their... love. Trembling hands. He stared at them now. Old too early, wise too late. Whose hands were they now. A badly broken up Doc Grady knocked on his door and stepped inside.

"Chief, we're ready"

Mulcahy stood up, adjusted his tie and fixed his tunic.

"Look okay" he asked

"Fine Chief" said Doc "Just fine"

But before they left, Augustine would wash his hands of at least one dirty deed. When the confession was over, he threw the file on the desk in front of them.

"They're all original reports, Derek. Once they've been done away with, the slate is clean. When this is over, I want you to put a match to this shit. For what I have done to you, to all of you, I am truly sorry. I will carry the guilt with me always. The money's there, every penny"

Doc patted his shoulder. He was a good man.

"Guilt's a destructive thing, Chief. It can rip you down." And he thought "Put a match to it. Now... let's do this" They threw open the great doors of Meadowvale and went to where the staff were waiting.

It was the loaves and the fishes. On the instructions of Delahunty, the jail only kept a handful of riot suits and batons were a rare commodity. But, as they stood there, in the early hours, they cut a fiercesome sight. Some wore helmets, others donned chest plates or limb guards, but the great bulk were uniformed, and though Augustine asked that they stayed out of it, they would not be deprived their dues. Their raw, pulsating anger would be their weapon and those who did not carry a truncheon, waved whatever means of battle they could find. Their ancestors had knocked the shite out of her Majesties forces withless, and a bunch of junkie scallywags were not going to stand in their way. Not tonight horse… not ever.

  Mulcahy cleared his throat and began.

"To our good friends of the Army and the Gardai, we thank you for your help and support on this awful day. But we would ask you to stand back now and let us fight our fight. We have all died a little here today, but the loss is ours and ours alone. So, stand back now and let us do what has to be done" When they had moved away, he addressed *his* people. "You will not be remembered outside these walls. Your names will not grace any memorial, you're hearts will not be eased by the world, but I tell you this" and it rose up in him "You are the bravest men and women that history will ever forget. You were, all of you, moulded by the wisdom of the jailer who fell tonight, and though his flame may be gone, his legacy will burn an inferno in your souls long after this day is done. You'll see it in each other, and if you are lucky, you'll see it in yourselves. Now comrades... let's take this stinking shithole back"

Throughout the day, Whacker Doyle had kept abreast of news bulletins on his radio. They gauged their infamy by the newsreaders tone, and in the moments after the 3am broadcast, they felt that they were legends. They heralded the nights butchery as Sean Talbots last noble act. One of the good guys, one of them, and, as they shook their fists and chanted his name, they were unaware of Leonard Fennell as he walked, alone, across the circle and unlocked the gates that led into the Blue wing.

It was Barry O Shea that heard it first. A rumble. Low. In the distance. Getting closer. Louder. Harder. Awesome. Deafening.

"FUCK ME" he screamed "THEY'RE COMING" and they were just about ready for war, when it came. There was an explosion of bodies, men, women, old, young, angry, *very fucking angry*, insane and unafraid, and they charged, with Mulcahy at the helm, into the chaos where they were met head on by the rabble. The mother of all jail battles, the battle for Meadowvale, had begun.

It was savage and unrelenting. Bodies dropped, blood spilled and all over, the sound of bone on crunching bone was only muffled slightly by the thunderous rhythm of cell doors being battered throughout the prison. It was the language of carnage, and it roared into the night like a wild animal. The jail was a living, breathing creature and the good folk of Meadowvale sat, terrified, in their beds and prayed for the boys and girls in the monsters belly. Wave after wave it came. Ground was lost to the beasts, but again and again and again they launched themselves forward and ripped into the black hearts of wicked men. And so they fought, under the long dark cloak of the witching hours.

By the time the dawn had broken, it was over. Ambulances sped through the main gate and firemen reeled out hoses and drowned the life from the last of the fires. Smoke billowed into the morning sky and formed a dirty great cloud above the place but, all in all, it was quiet. Officers, bloodied and blackened, staggered out onto the steps and collapsed. Chief fire officer, Christy Maguire, organised his teams and they darted from warder to warder tending wounds. Tragically, for the brigade, this was just another days work. A constant stream of Officers dropped where they stood. Some sat up, others did not bother. The fact that they had regained control of the jail meant nothing. They certainly didn't feel in control. They didn't feel anything. Numbed and shocked, they would have cried if they could but they couldn't. What the fuck, they had a lifetime ahead for that. Doc Grady and Augustine Mulcahy breached the barriers across the entrance to the old tradesmens tunnel and shuffled down to the store room door. A Garda forensics team were at work, and they were told to stay outside so as not to compromise the integrity of the crime scene. There was *no* integrity here, and, as if to prove it, a pair of childs trousers was bagged as evidence. They stood there in silence and stared in. In time they would find themselves down here often, reliving the horror of that fateful night. But the outcome would always be the same and there was nothing anybody could ever do to change that.

At lunchtime that day, Gerard Magner, sneaked out of his house and skirted to the shop. He had not been present for the ordeal due to a mystery illness that had now, thankfully, cleared up, but he caught it on the news. Nasty business, he thought. He was glad that he had made alternative arrangements, and, should everything go to plan, he would pack in the jail for the property game full time. As he made his way through the back streets to the corner store, he was interrupted by Pablo Rogers.

"Ah, there you are now" he said "We were all worried about you... weren't we lads"

Matty Morris, Doc Grady and The Movieland Twins stepped into view.

"Indeed we were" said Matty "We all thought you were up to something"

"And why did we think that, boys?" asked Ollie

"Because of those" said Mick. Doc held up the letters and pointed to the tourist board logo.

"So, you're in the guesthouse business now" said Derek "I hope there'll be specials for the lads, you scumbag" and he was still amazed at Magners greed.

Ger made a run for it, and he was well down the road when Victor Roberts tripped him up. "I didn't mean it" Magner was shouting when they surrounded him "Jesus have mercy on me"

"Calm down for fuck sake" said Doc "We can do a deal. Shur, aren't you one of us"

Ger was relieved "Yes… yes… a deal." He was saying "I'll cut you all in. There's enough for everyone"

Victor made a lunge, but Pablo stopped him.

"Look" said Doc "we have a business proposition for you. It concerns the yank"

Ger was confused. "The fucking yank?"

"hmmm… he's interested in that plot of yours, Rio Grande" and they laughed "There was some disagreement about value, I understand. Well, we put our heads together and we reckon it's worth about… … two grand. How does that grab you" and he produced the cash.

"That's my money, you thieving bastard"

"Correct" said Doc "Now, you can use that money as an incentive to donate a little gift to our American friend, or if you so wish, you can use it as bail money, because you *are* going away my friend, and for a very long time. But, shur, we'll look after you when you come in, wont we lads" and they all muttered in agreement.

Magner was distraught. Rio Grande might have been worth a few bob in the right circles. But, as he stared at them, at their bruises, the alternative was nightmarish.

"Alright" he said "you win"

"Good lad, Ger" said Pablo "Now run along and get those deeds"

When he returned, they did the deal. It was agreed that if Magner ever raised the issue again, they would shop him to the Gardai. There would be no problems. "Oh, there is one other thing" said Doc "Your friend, David Orr, not a word to him about this. I want you to contact him and tell him to be here on Wednesday at 2pm. If he isn't, we'll take it that you blabbed and we'll kick the shit out of you. Do you understand?"

"Sure... I understand"

"You can be such a *nice* man Ger" said Matty and he turned to Doc "Are you sure about this?"

"Yeah, I see what you mean" said Doc "ah fuck it" and they kicked the shit out of him anyway.

Bradford Shaw was gobsmacked. The ancestral home was his? He could not believe it. What kind of man was Magner. One minute he is trying to screw him over Rio Grande, the next minute he is giving it to him for nothing. Figure that one out. He asked Pablo to explain it again.

"Like I said, the guy walks into the jail this morning and just falls to bits at the sight of the place. He starts babbling on about how people are more important than possessions, and he keeps calling out your name. I think it was his good deed in a dark and weary world. After that, he hands over the deeds and tells us to sort out the paperwork with you. That's all I know"

Shaw could not keep a straight face. "Are you for real? You boys all did something to that guy, I just know it. What'ya do, beat him up?"

Pablo shrugged. "Whatever, the place is yours now. We both know you belong here. Any way I'm not so sure those people outside are going to let you leave"

The crowds had gathered to touch 'The miracle man' and they were here to stay. Earlier, Councillor Paddy Harte, had called round to find out if Shaw would go on the towns books. A good steady wage to stay public, show off a little of what the Lord had granted him. It was good for tourism. The town needed him. He said that he would have to think about it. Nora Hegarty had already signed Sean up. Paddy had agreed to write up a contract, and one of the stipulations demanded that Meadowvale would support Sean in the event of her death. He *would* be taken care of, that was good enough for her. Shaw took the deeds.

"The dog stays" he said.

Pablo watched as the General moved unsteadily.

"I'm confused, Brad" and you could have heard it "Was there a miracle or not?"

"Well, look at it this way. I came over here in a wheelchair and now I'm on my feet. Mrs. Hegarty, as I understand, was about to lose her son. Now, the man is a fuckin' celebrity and the town *couldn't* lose him. So Paul… you tell me"

On Wednesday, David Orr swaggered into town, unaware of the early mornings events. He had heard about the riot, but the details of the healing were sketchy at best. He was not in the place five minutes, when Victor stopped him on the street. Roberts could not believe his luck, it seemed, as he was about to contact Orr that very afternoon.

"Nora's ready to do business" he said "I think she realises that you were right. Poor aul' Sean will be lost when she goes and she may as well put him into decent care now. It would be an easier transition for him if she's still around"

Orr happily escorted Victor to the guesthouse. Roberts left him in the kitchen while he went to get herself. The bastard was delighted and he took the opportunity to get a closer look at his new venture. He was taking notes on the décor when he was startled by Mrs. Hegarty. She stood in the doorway, like a Picasso. Her black lace brassiere hugged her ample bosom and her matching panties were lost beneath the great expanse of her flesh. The smoke rings of a fine Cuban cigar drifted past her face and her eyes were obscured by the rubber cat mask that she was wearing.

"Hello Tiger" she purred and she clawed the air.

"MRS. HEGARTY" Orr gasped "YOU'RE POSITIVELY INDECENT"

Victor Roberts appeared behind her dressed only in a leather pouch.

"Not at all, son. She's as decent as they come... when you know her well enough" and he grinned at Orr before he kissed her.

This was insane. Outrageous. But as he attempted to leave, Victor grabbed him and hoisted him off the ground. Nora opened the living room door and Roberts threw him inside. He landed in a heap. When he lifted his head, he was overcome with fear. A large, thonged man was tied over a beer barrel, and though he looked terrified, his protestations were muffled by the Granny Smith that was wedged into his mouth. Two other men in Y-fronts and riding boots, took turns at spanking the leather stringed buttocks of their victim, and Big Tom and the Mainliners belted out 'The Old Rustic Bridge' on the gramophone. In the corner, a dejected Ger Magner crouched in a floral patterned dress, with a sign that read WE'VE BEEN HAD.

"You'll never get away with this" shouted Orr "I'll get the guards" at which point the gentleman on the barrel, spat out the apple, smiled and said

"Sergeant Peter O Driscoll at your service. How can I be of help?"

Orr lost it. He screamed and cried out, and they had to whack him several times to calm him down. When he was more relaxed, and the blood had been wiped away, Victor brought him up to date.

"We have you and Shirley Temple by the short and curlies, son. Now, this is what we're going to do. You will ring your office and say that a mistake was made in relation to Sean Hegarty, that no actual complaints were filed against the lad, that you accept full responsibility for the error, and that you wish to tender your resignation with immediate effect. In return, no charges will be filed in relation to this incident and you can fuck off out of here a free man"

It was done. The Movieland Twins released O Driscoll, much to his disappointment, and Magner was allowed to join them.

"Now Mr. Orr" Nora grinned "You'll stay for tea and sangwidges", and a pair of rubber long johns were thrown at him.

# CHAPTER FIVE: THURSDAY

(i)     **THE LAST WALTZ**

The old church of Drumasheen was a fitting temple for Dinnys farewell. Every night since 1993, every night bar one, he had lit those candles, and as a mark of respect only four flames flickered throughout the service. Speakers were erected outside for the throngs of mourners and well wishers who could not find a space inside, and the chapel was packed not only with the men and women of Meadowvale, but with uniformed Officers from every penal institution in the land. If Denis O Brien had made the road easy for hundreds in his life, they were here today to do the same for him in death. General Bradford Shaw leaned on his cane and, in full military dress, he made his way to the casket, where he removed his Congressional Medal of Honour and placed it with by the wreaths.

The jail choir was fronted by Aine Devlin, a large lady from cork whose voice was so sweet, it was once said of her, that warders did not mind dying if Aine sang at their funeral. When the hush settled upon them, she sang Puccinis 'O Mio Babbino Caro', as one by one, they touched the tri colour and paid their last respects.

During mass, Veronica Gilmore was assisted to the altar by Matty Morris and Pablo Rogers. In one of the most emotional scenes ever witnessed in the town, she struggled her way through a poem she had written in the sombre lonesomes of his passing.

*You are gone now,*
*all is quiet,*
*in the stillness of eternal night,*
*but as I wake,*
*to mornings flame,*
*I find I'm calling out your name,*
*And reaching out,*
*To touch your hair,*
*with loving hands but you're no there.*
*Now Summers gone,*
*And Winter's in,*
*forever,*
*till we meet again.*

They cried openly everywhere, for it was all they could do.

Jean Cooke held her husband. For them, they're would be better days, new beginnings, but as Augustine and Eileen Mulcahy sat on either side of their son, they knew that there were many rivers to cross before the nightmare was finally over. Conor was lost to them, sealed behind the expressionless eyes of butchered innocence... a prisoner there. Augustine asked for the strength to find him. Nora Hegarty and Victor Roberts stood in the open air and enjoyed the freedom of Seans spirit. They *would* love him always.

The guard of honour marched in slow advance along the aisle to the coffin. They were led by Paul and Philip Drennan, officers and brothers who had stood together in the Lebanon as they did in the jails, as they did in their own lives. They were a symbol of the unity that existed in the ranks and, on their command, Denis O Brien was lifted shoulder high and carried out with all the dignity and respect that such a man deserved. A lone piper paved the way, and a multitude in mourning braved the harsh wind and made their way to the cemetery on Dinnegans Hump, where Dinny O Brien was laid to rest.

They did not see them as they left. Their eyes were too full of grief. But they strayed behind the mourners path on that grey Autumn day. Her blonde curls danced along the shoulders of her red dress and her pale blue eyes sparkled in the gloom. He was young and handsome and lean, and they linked hands as they waltzed across the trail, laughing as they went.

(ii)  FULL CIRCLE

A week ago Andrew Purcell had run from the 'Percival Richards Bar and Tavern', and disappeared back into the world. Just one fucking week ago. On that day, no one could have forseen the events that would unfold, or indeed, sense the change that was coming. They had kicked up their heels and faced life the jailer way. But now, today, they could not face anything. They were all burned out. They sat in silence and they drank alone. Percy busied himself behind the bar, and though he was glad of the respite, he had liked Dinny. He was a gentle man. The drink was free for now, but they would have to understand that it was only for now. Still, they were a sorry sight and he did not begrudge them the moment.

Shortly after 1pm, Augustine Mulcahy came into the pub in full uniform. He stood at the head of the bar and he stared into each face from beneath the lacquered peak of his Chiefs cap. Doc Grady thought to himself that if Mulcahy had come here to berate the men, he would want to fuck off out of it and save himself the hassle. Similar thoughts crossed the minds of the others. The Chief had come out of this with the huge respect of the men, but if he said one word, just one fucking word, then that was it.

He walked past them to the drinks display and pointed by Richards to a bottle of Glenfiddich.

"I'll have that, whatever it is" and he held the glass awkwardly before he threw it back. Then, to Percys shock and dismay, as Mulcahy climbed onto the bar counter, threw his cap to the crowd, and began unbuckling his trousers... the place went up.

# EPILOGUE: TIME AFTER TIME

JULY 7th 1813

Paudie Mulhare was tired. He sat outside his shebeen, on the slopes of the hump, and rested in the evening sun. Beyond the rhythmic popping of his bubbling cauldron, he could hear the mumbles and mutters of a rosary congregation and, further down the valley, a procession of candle waving Christians ambled silently behind a huge wooden crucifix on its way to the chapel. Shortly after 7pm, he was joined by Seanie Maguire. Sean had staggered from the bushes in an awful state. He'd been badly scratched and he had, what appeared to be, goat bites to his hands and face. He had not shaved in some time and wild ginger strands shot in all directions from his jaw line. His trousers had been hastily donned, and the fact that they were on inside out, did not seem to bother him at all. And he had been grazing again in Widow McCormacks field. Half chewed clumps of grass clung to his lips and there was a green hue to his complexion.

On putting a safe distance between himself and the bush from whence he came, he shouted "Filthy animals" and an angry creature bleated in response. The trousers lost their grip on him and plummeted past his knees, trapping his ankles and sending him crashing to the ground beside Paudie.

"Oh Jesus Christ, can you ever forgive me?" was his plea and it was an earnest submission.

There were a few moments of fumbling before Maguire was aware that he was in company. He scrutinised Paudie intensely through Poteen shot eyes, before he burst into tears. He lifted himself, unsteadily, to his knees and he bowed his head.

"Bless me father" he began "for I have sinned. I have been a bad man, Father, a *very* bad man indeed"

Paudie Mulhare looked all around him to make sure that they were alone. They were, and Seanie *was* talking to him.

"Seanie" he said "Tis me... Paudie"

Maguire looked up. "Paudie?"

"Yes"

"Paudie?" he said again.

"Yes, yes, Paudie Mulhare. Will you get a grip, man?"

Once again Seanie burst into tears. "Paudie Mulhare... will *you* hear my confession?"

"I will not" said Paudie, and he started down the hump in a trot with Maguire close behind.

As they neared the base of the hill, Seanie gave up the chase and held his arms outstretched. "Will nobody love *me*?" he shouted with such desperation that Mulhare almost came back. But they had stumbled across the rosary crew and, on seeing Maguires divine appearance, Bridget Casey went pale and wane, and declared to all present that the good Lord was among them. Seanie was swamped.

Fiery clouds climbed up from the horizon and painted the evening sky ahead of Paudie. He did not like the look of them. He did not like the look of them one bit. His mother, God rest her, had always told him that such a celestial display was a foreboding. Change was coming to Meadowvale, and not necessarily for the good. In a moment of clarity, he thought that bad things would happen to good people in this very place, and he had a sudden fear that he may be included in whatever reformation was afoot. By the time he reached his own doorstep, he was sure that destiny would not be kind to him this night. He had a strong compulsion to protect the recipe. That would be his heirloom, he felt, and at some new dawn in history, a man of his blood would travel oceans to claim it. He took the sacred parchment from his tobacco bowl and, lifting the great stone from the hearth of the fireplace, he laid it there with the coppers and pence he had banked in the earth.

"Should I not greet another day" he said "some future generation will revel in your charms"

He moved the boulder back in place, and went to answer a knock at his door.

Bradford Shaw woke from a heavy sleep. He was groggy. His night had been filled with strange dreams and there were voices, voices that called out to him from distant lands. Now that he was up, he could not recall their message and the forces that had carried him from his bed were faded and vague. But he was left with an overwhelming sense of place, a powerful rush of belonging... and an unshakeable urge to dig.

ISBN 1412024439